THE
KENSINGTON
REPTILARIUM

A Random House book
Published by Random House Australia Pty Ltd
Level 3, 100 Pacific Highway, North Sydney NSW 2060
www.randomhouse.com.au

First published by Random House Australia in 2013

Addresses for companies within the Random House Group can be found at
www.randomhouse.com.au/offices.

National Library of Australia
Cataloguing-in-Publication Entry

Author: Gemmell, N.J.
Title: The Kensington reptilarium / N.J. Gemmell
ISBN: 978 0 85798 050 2 (pbk)
Dewey Number: A823.3

Cover design and illustration by Allison Colpoys
Internal design and illustration by Allison Colpoys
Typeset by Midland Typesetters, Australia
Printed in Australia by Griffin Press, an accredited ISO AS/NZS 14001:2004
Environmental Management System printer

Random House Australia uses papers that are natural, renewable and recyclable
products and made from wood grown in sustainable forests. The logging
and manufacturing processes are expected to conform to the environmental
regulations of the country of origin.

THE KENSINGTON REPTILARIUM

N.J. GEMMELL

RANDOM HOUSE AUSTRALIA

BASTI

KICK

SCRUFF

BERT

PIN

BUCKET

and Banjo!

To Lachie, Ollie, Thea and Jago

1

A BET

'How long do you reckon it'd take to fry an egg on Matilda's bonnet?'

Scruff is looking longingly at our car, which is already boiling hot in the 44-degree heat – and it's only nine a.m.

'Fifty-two seconds!' Bert rises to the challenge. 'Do it, Scruffy boy, come on. *Anything* would be better than Kick's cooking.' She shoots a glance at me, knowing I'll take the bait. Which I most certainly do.

'Just *you* try being a mum plus a dad around here, young lady.' I poke out my tongue. Everyone knows that any experiment at being a grown-up ended months ago. 'Twenty-nine seconds,' I exclaim, 'and not a fly's fart more!'

My attempt at breakfast – a frypan with a rug of eggs tastefully congealed on its bottom – is grabbed and said eggs are flung wide into the yard. They spin like a dinner plate. Land – plop! – in the red dust.

Cooking. Pah. I give up. I've had enough of it.

Our dog, Bucket, scoots for the mess of the breakfast and gobbles it up. I bow to her exquisite taste. 'Well, at least *someone* appreciates me around here.'

Then I stand on the table in my leather flying cap, fix Mum's old driving goggles firmly over my eyes, straighten my back and salute.

'Troops, as of this moment I hereby resign from the positions of cook, cleaner, mother, father, storyteller, governess, putterer-to-bed, chief hunter, nose-wiper, Pin-tracker, master spy and war general. You're free. The whole blinkin' lot of you! I'm off.'

'Yaaaaaaay!'

My three siblings – Scruff, eleven, Bert, nine, and Pin, four – hoot with glee and do an instant war dance; Bucket joins in for good measure with a great flurry of leaps and barks. A finger's waggled at her. I expect mutiny in the ranks from the humans who inhabit this adult-forsaken place but not from our dingo we've raised since a pup. Obediently she sits and pants. That's better. I wink my thanks.

'Forty-eight seconds, girls. The bet's on!' Scruff sings, rushing to the larder to gather more eggs. Dad left him his old wristwatch from World War I, complete with its stopwatch, and he's been timing the entire world ever since.

'Twelve eleven! Twelve eleven!' Pin exclaims.

This is the biggest number he knows, and, er, as you can see, I've been a bit slack in the governess department of late. We'll get to numbers one day.

We all scramble out to Matilda, our trusty car, which I can drive (with three blocks of wood tied with ropes to the pedals and a pillow on the seat) at the grand old age of thirteen, thank you very much.

'A minute's silence please.' Bert clasps her chest dramatically when we get there (ever the drama queen). She raises her head to the wide blue heavens. Bucket takes her place behind the wheel. 'Please bring Daddy back to us by Christmas Eve. With the following: a rifle for Scruff, a slingshot for Pin, a black velvet dress from Paris for me and a . . . a little . . . *book* . . . of some sort . . . for the ex-governess.' She wrinkles her nose in distaste in my direction.

My eyes narrow. 'Dinner's all yours, Madame Pompadour. Tonight. Just see what *you* can do with a roo tail, two cups of flour and a chocolate bar.'

'Forty-eight seconds, ladies!' Scruff exclaims, ever the peacemaker, his palms wide between both of us as he scrutinises the tall blue sky.

We all do. Oh, it'll deliver all right. Cook those eggs in the blink of an eye. Because we live smack bang in the middle of the hottest place on earth – the Central Australian desert. And we live here, at the moment, all by our glorious selves.

Dad's gone away on yet another of his expeditions. He's always heading off, ever since I could talk he's been disappearing and then coming back with a great wallop of presents and stories about princes and paupers, India and Ceylon and Paris, samurai swords and civil war muskets, spies and saboteurs, crocs and stingrays and sharks. He's an adventure hunter, that's all we know, liberating peoples and animals across the world, and it's always of the highest importance and the most mysterious intelligence. His latest mission: yep, you guessed it, top secret. But it's to save the world from imminent destruction – even though the war, er, ended several months ago. Apparently. We've spent World War II on our station in the middle of Woop Woop, scouring the horizon for Japs, which always turn into camels as they get close through the haze of heat. But we're ready for 'em!

And Mum? She died when Pin was born; Dad says she ran away to God, because another little Caddy surprise was just too shocking for this world to ever cope with and she needed to instruct God how to do it. Mum's always up there, with us, close, we must never forget it.

The four of us climb onto Matilda's bonnet, which creaks companionably with our weight but never gives, thank goodness, 'cause we're on here a lot. Our darling, faithful old girl of a ute, she's taken us to every waterhole within a hundred-mile radius thanks to Dad. She's sped between sand dunes trailing an old mattress that we've all clung onto for dear life, she's carried swags and firewood and dead roos and goannas piled high for feasts, as well as endless gaggles of kids on hunting expeditions with our blackfella mates.

Dad organised for Aunty Ethel to stay with us during this latest absence – something about me 'becoming a woman and needing some help', which he couldn't talk about, and he would blush whenever I tried to ask, but excuse me, I'm more than all right now, thank you very much. I've got his war pistol and his whip, his car key and a stash of books – what more does a girl need?

Aunty Ethel agreed that her services might no longer be required after she found the entire occupants of Bert's scorpion farm in her sheets. Which came the day after Pin whacked Scruff with a fresh roo tail and sprayed blood across Aunty Ethel's white Sunday-best dress, and Scruff used her glasses to set fire to the straw under the chook house as a liberation experiment.

'Your father was always the black sheep of the family – but he's got nothing on you lot,' she'd said as she slammed the door of her car. 'I'll write and tell him to get back instantly. No one else will have you. Kick, you'll just just have to work out how to become a lady all by yourself. And clean up that potty mouth of yours, because your father certainly won't!'

The last sight of our visitor from hoity toity down south: her Morris Minor coughing and spluttering as it disappeared in a cloud of dust.

Excellent. That's how we like it. We rubbed our hands in glee. Me free to do and say what I want. Kids free of supervision and baths. Plus the most superb development of the lot: Dad on his way back to look after us.

Except he's not here. Yet.

And it's been an awfully long time. Every day we expect him to arrive. The days are ticking on, the tins are running low, as well as the powdered milk and flour with too many weevils in it, and Christmas is in a week, the bush pine will have to be selected and chopped and Dad's always in command of that. Along with bagging the bush turkey, tuning the piano for the singalong, directing the Christmas pantomine (sole audience member: Bucket), and painting across the entire tin roof, in bright red, our yearly message to Santa on his flying kangaroos in case he misses it: 'STOP! BEER + GOOD KIDS HERE.'

'Ah, shouldn't that be written the other way round?' Scruff had asked last year.

'In this heat,' Dad had laughed, 'Father Christmas needs a beer before anything,' and clapped his son on the back.

'I do too!' Scruff had jumped in right quick.

'You're only ten, mate. I'll tell you what. I'll give you one when you've grown some hairs on your chest – and you're all of eleven.' Then they'd both cackled with laughter that wouldn't stop. Little boys, both of them, especially on December 25th. So. Scruff's come of age now and Dad needs to hurry up. Any moment, I just know it, can feel it.

Dad Junior now holds an egg high. 'Troops, are we ready? Steady?'

Pin holds my hand, squeezes with excitement.

Bert examines her nails, which she's just covered with old blackboard paint that's still hanging around, miraculously, even though all the governesses have long fled. 'Excuse me, stop. We're not ready yet because I have a question. A crucial one. What does the winner get?'

Scruff looks at her, thinking. It'll be something to do with warfare, I bet. 'My entire grenade collection.'

'Do any of them work?' Bert's now looking straight at me, planning her attack.

That'd be right. Just because I told her she has to pull her weight and help with a week's worth of dishes now that we have nothing left to eat off.

'Not a single one, sis!' Scruff cackles then cracks the egg with great aplomb between his spread legs. 'Breakfast is on its way, ladies and gentleman – the best feast you have ever tasted in your life!' He counts from his watch, 'One – two – three – four –'

Pin's tugging me, trying to get me off the car. 'Sssh,' I tell him, 'don't interrupt, pup.'

'But Kicky . . .' he whines.

'Twelve – eleven –' Scruff winks at Pin '– thirteen – fourteen –'

But Pin's head is somewhere else. Our little man can be distracted by an ant, a fly, anything but the task at hand, and that usually leads to him wandering off, which always gives us heart attacks. Right on

cue he jumps from Matilda. Heads to the front gate.
Our gaze follows him.

To an enormous plume of angry red dust, bulleting
straight at us from the horizon.

The egg is forgotten as we rush to Pin . . . hearts
in our mouths.

What is it?

It's not Dad, it's too fast. It's something else.

2

WE ARE
INVADED

**Right. This is the weirdest day of my life and I
think it's only going to get weirder.**

A police car. Coming straight at us with its big
plume of dust. The worst car possible. Because
it means something not very good. Snatchings.
Removal. Punishment. Too many questions, too
much suspicion. But it slows, then stops a couple of
hundred yards away, as if it's scared (as it should be)
of what goes on in these parts. Scared of the four
of us with our big reputation that's got everyone –
including Aunty Ethel – running for the hills. As if
there's a big huge warning sign at our gate:

The police car starts up again. Revs hard like a bull about to charge. I'm feeling sick. Because this is only the start of what's coming next and this car looks mean like a grenade looks mean, as if it doesn't like four kids alone without their parents in the middle of the toughest desert on earth, as if it has to put a stop to this.

I blast hard on Dad's trench whistle that's always around my neck – it once saved him from a Turk's bullet ripping through his chest and it's going to save us now, just watch.

'Action stations! Invasion imm-in-ent!'

So. Let this battle commence. We've scared off everyone else. Because if we're taken from here we won't be coming back, I just know it, I've read too many books: they'll put us in a home with high walls and rats and Dad'll return from his expedition to an empty house and a skeleton of Bucket by his bed and we promised to look after everything and we'll have let him down and no, oh no, we're not doing that. We've got Dad's arsenal of souvenirs from all his adventures, a mighty war chest in fact: Japanese swords and Javanese knives, Burmese shields and Thai bayonets, fishing nets from Sumatra and balloon silk from India, not to mention ropes. Twenty-eight types.

We all know the drill. We've discussed it enough. In thirty seconds flat we're in our places.

Scruff – lover of bets, pranks, cooking and fights and the best shot in these parts – clangs the gate shut (well, as shut as he can get with its broken latch) then, with a bow and arrows slung across his shoulder and a sling through his belt, he scrambles up the flying fox so he can zip across the driveway as soon as the car's in range and slingshot all his marbles and Dad's entire rock collection smack bang into an unsuspecting windscreen.

Bert – lover of graves, cupboards, fashion and all things black – is actually staying bold in the light. This must be serious (and miraculously, we're in agreement for once). Our little ball of fury stands poised by the barricade of sharpened, slanting sticks that we've erected across the front of the gate as extra protection. She's armed with her picnic basket of rotten eggs kept just for these moments and her top three attack-scorpions in their chocolate tin, plus an extra special surprise in the pyjama sack she fashioned from the second-best tablecloth.

Pin, mighty Pin, is on the verandah holding back a wildly barking Bucket by hugging her around the neck until the crucial moment when whoever it is steps out of their car and bam! – Pin will let go and they won't know what's hit 'em. Our girl's the wildest, snarliest dingo in the west when she wants to be, and I'm talking dog here, not sister – well, both, actually – and Pin adores them equally and clings like crazy to each.

And then yours truly. Directing the lot of them. Up in the crow's nest (Mum's old laundry basket) high on the rooftop, hidden behind the chimney with its parasol and two upside-down wellies poking out – our grim warning to anyone getting too close. One hand is tight around a bucket of flat riverbed stones; the other around the slingshot from a ghost gum that's never let me down yet. I've got a mighty arsenal of attack-objects here – collected over the years to help us out with any invasions from the world beyond. Which is now.

The police car smashes through our barricade. It scatters like an army of skittles. Right. I give three sharp whistles. Meaning: direst threat. Meaning: close. Dad's hunting rifle is grabbed – his third-best, the one he left for us without Aunty Ethel knowing, only to be used in the most terrifying of circumstances.

Bert lobs an egg dead centre at the windscreen; Scruff lets loose an assault of marbles from the flying fox. Pin releases Bucket's collar and in a flurry of snarl our girl races to the car trying to savage its door handle off. Bert hurls the last of her eggs then grabs Millie the sand snake from her pyjama sack ready for a freshly vacated car seat; we're calling up the entire troops but still the car comes and comes.

I aim for the front tyre – got it. There's only one crack shot better than Scruff in this place and it's a girl, yes a girl, not that he'd ever admit it.

The car spins wildly. Oops. Almost crashes into the house. Double oops. Out races a policeman with pistol in hands and – what? – he seems to know exactly where to aim. Straight at the roof. That would be me. No. Don't you dare, mate.

'Thomasina, raise your hands above your head and come out. No funny business, madam. We've got you in our sights.'

Who says it's me up here? And the name's Kick, thank you very much. That Thomasina malarkey is lost in the mists of time; Dad'll back me up on this. Thomasina will get you nowhere, mate.

'I know it's you . . . Kick.'

Great.

'Ralph. Albertina. Phineas,' he yells, and everyone else is now cringing at the full horror of their proper names. 'Don't do *anything* your father wouldn't be proud of.'

Dead silence. Everyone waiting for . . . me. Er, right.

Nup. Not biting, mister. They'll have to haul me out in a box from this place. A sharp whistle blow – the signal to the troops to regroup, fight on.

Bucket crouches before the man, growls; waiting for the attack command, my whistle like a whipbird. I slide down the slippery dip from the roof to the backyard, land on the mattress in a cloud of dust and race through the house and hide by the doorless front door, hunting rifle poised. Eyes to Scruff's double peephole that's been gouged into the wall with Dad's penknife precisely for moments like this. The last stand. Too much to lose here: a house, freedom, a father's return, an arsenal of ancient weapons, the right to wear trousers and cuss, brothers and even a sister.

Trigger, gently pressed. Stillness. As if the entire desert is listening in.

Splat.

An egg. Right across the policeman's face. Great. Bert squeals in triumph from the water tower. I groan. Now they know where she is. Good one, girl.

The policeman wipes the egg from his eyes. 'You have a very special visitor, you lot. With some important news.'

Eh? Wasn't expecting that. The pistol's lowered.

Bert's suddenly transfixed; no more eggs. The car door opens. Out steps . . . slowly . . . a foot in a very shiny shoe . . . a leg in a very white suit . . . a new person entirely. He doesn't belong in this car. This desert. This dirt. And it's like he's kind of . . . squirming. He steps into the dust like he doesn't quite trust it; as if he's been told there are deadly snakes everywhere, which of course there are but not in the open, silly, any bushy knows that, which you obviously aren't.

Splat.

Another egg. It's as if the entire desert sucks in its breath.

'*Alber-TINA,*' I whisper in fury, like I do ten thousand times a day in my life.

'Now *that's* a greeting.' The man stares down at his freshly yolked suit. Nice work, girl, dead centre. Perfect in every respect.

We've never been invaded by a white suit before. I peer around the doorframe with the field glasses. Hmm. Skin that can't cope with sun, shoes that've never seen dirt, hands that've never skinned a roo let alone held the gun that shot one.

I glance at Bert and Scruff, now both up in the water tower and covered from head to foot in red dust with crazy stick-up hair and rag clothes held on with twine and ochre smears like wild Indian paint and bare feet as tough as old boots; lordy, they look like some feral species of bird up there, spawned by another planet entirely. Wild, untameable, alone, oh yes – and never being dragged from this place that sings in our blood and our bones.

'The war is over,' the Suit declares.

Silence.

'We won. Perhaps you haven't heard.'

Well. Okay. We did know something of this and if you expect cheering it's not going to work because in these parts the big shebang up north has barely registered except that it took away all the cattle to feed the troops; and Dad, every now and then, on his secret missions and he'd always come back crammed with tall tales about Nazis and B-52s and the Luftwaffe and the Blitz.

'There's something else . . .' the Suit says.

17

Don't want to know, mister. I fire the rifle two feet above his head. We will not be taken from here, we will not. The sound pings through the desert sky. The man doesn't flinch. Hmm.

'Kick.' The policeman's losing patience. 'You need to hear this.' A sigh. 'In person.'

I lower the pistol. Because the way this policeman's speaking suggests this might well be the toughest thing he's ever had to do in his life. It's in his voice. Bucket suddenly sits before the man, utterly still, poised.

'It's about your father . . .'

A cry from the water tower, abruptly cut off, as if a hand's been slammed across a mouth.

The Suit takes off his hat. 'I've come all the way across the world to speak to you.'

Right. So. They're all waiting for me. Even Bucket. It could be a trick.

Our dingo girl makes a decision. She pads across to the strange new man, turns and looks straight into me. As if to say 'come on, *you*'. The man holds her face close and whispers something. Bucket whimpers, licks him.

My mouth's suddenly dry, I'm breathing hard, can't move. What's he saying? And then – hang on – three apparitions slowly emerge before the men, covered in red dust, weapons lowered. Disorder in the ranks! *They're not meant to do this.* There'll be hell to pay later. Stop, troops, stop!

'Kick?' the policeman yells. 'We're just waiting for you now. And then we can commence.'

Can't. Stuck. Because tears are suddenly pricking my eyes. Furiously I smear them off; too old for this. Can't make them stop. But I've got a reputation to maintain here, the fiercest one of the lot, *no one* can see me like this.

'Man to man. Woman to man. *Girl* to man,' blusters the Suit.

I spit in frustration. Bucket's looking straight at me. Scruff too, needing his mate to say what's next because we're a team, all four of us, and this needs sorting out. Bert starts to plead 'Kicky' over and over like we're suddenly best friends. No one's noticing Pin, who's wandering off as fast as his dear pudgy legs can carry him. It's his party trick, he's always getting lost because his curiosity is endless and boundless, to Dad's infinite delight, but he's about to disappear out the gate into – great, guys – the deadliest desert on earth.

Turn, you lot, turn! *Grab him.*

Right. Obviously I won't be resigning from parenthood at this exact point. Absolutely hopeless, the lot of you.

I drop the rifle and stride from the house into the hurting glare, one enormous scowl of indignation, and march straight past them to little Pin toddling along, oblivious. He's our medieval kissing post, we all gravitate to him for cuddles and snuggles and giggles and I'm not about to lose him now, his job is too important. I grab his hand, he's all squealy and squirmy, and swing him around. 'Kicky! Kicky!' he chortles. But the ferociousness of the grip soon stills him down.

Big breath.

I face the lot of them, fierce. Bucket comes up to me and I find the softness of her ear and caress it over and over. 'What's up, mate?' I whisper and she's licking away the smear of tears like she knows why they've been there and why they're going to be there for years to come. My heart's suddenly tight in my chest as if a great fist is squeezing it.

The Suit mops his face with his hanky. Clears his throat.

It's Bucket's cue: she jumps up right at him and leaves red paw prints smeared across that crazily clean linen. The man yelps in horror, steps back, drops his hanky; Bert dashes forward and plops it on her head. That'd be right. Always desperate for something new, anything she can grab, especially

20

if she can wear it and turn it into high-fashion fabulousness and believe me, out here we don't see much that's clean and shiny and city. Which is this stranger all over.

'Bucky, Bert, *down*,' but no one's listening and it's now just a big crazy mess of barking dog and squealing kid and dust and the Suit's trying to say something but no one's catching it and I've got a straining dog in one hand and a straining girl in the other and Pin's all rabbity behind us and there's only one way to describe this chaos: sheer, utter, typical Caddy madnesss.

'I *said*,' the Suit is suddenly declaring, 'my name is Horatio Smythe-Hippet, the *Honourable*, and I'd like to extend to this most esteemed, er –' he doesn't quite know what '– gathering . . . my sincere and utmost –' a breath '– sympathy.'

What's he saying? Scruff's not paying attention, itching to try his slingshot, just a tiny pebble, soft, right on that city shin – I can read him like a book – and this Horatio Something Something's speaking in a voice we can't get our heads around and oh my goodness we're all suddenly transfixed because a fly's just about to go into his mou–

Yep. It's in. Bingo. He shuts his lips in horror. Blows out his cheeks. A huge gulp. We laugh.

'They're good for you,' Scruff offers helpfully. 'Full of protein.'

Horatio looks helplessly at the officer. 'I'm not sure how to proceed,' he says, and thrusts some big thick envelope at me that has 'official' stained all over it. 'I'm frightfully sorry.'

It's like a candle's suddenly been blown out.

3
AN OFFER

Everything is very, very still.

'I regret to in-inform –' I start reading aloud all wobbly then can't go on because the words are dancing, swimming on the page, and Horatio takes the paper with a sudden, startling gentleness. I look up at him. Drop slowly down to Bucket and hold her tight and she licks my cheeks like she's saying come on, girl, stand up straight, be the head of the family because you must.

Horatio looks around. 'I think it's best just to carry on, eh?'

And so he does. In a new silence entirely. Because there's an awful stop. To everything.

Dad is missing.

Vanished.

It doesn't look good.

Horatio tells us that the only clue to what happened is a note on a ragged piece of yellow paper that was pinned by his hunting knife to a tree trunk somewhere up Woop Woop and he indicates north, vaguely, which means anywhere really — and what happened to the big adventure to save the world? Did Dad even begin it? Did he get diverted on the way by the thought of a monster croc? He's always wanted to find the biggest one in the world, he's told me that. My head's hurting, trying to work it all out. Can't. Horatio's explaining that the note's only just been found and who knows how long it's been there, who knows anything any more.

It's in Dad's lovely handwriting, neat when so much of him wasn't, like all the letters are standing to attention:

I love you so much, my little CRAZIES.
Not saying which of you is the
favourite—Haha. I'll tell you when
I see you!
It's another adventure. Gone ever so
slightly wrong. But I'll make it right.
You know me.
Be good. Do me proud. Laugh often.
Make me laugh too.
Can't wait to hear all of your stories.
And go now and live with someone who
needs you as much as you need him.
It's your Uncle Basti at the Kensington
Reptilarium. All right? (Because I
said, Kicketty. Don't ask, don't scowl,
don't raise your slingshot.)
Until I can get back to

The note stops bang, right there. Scruff's taking huge gulps of air like he can't breathe properly. Bert's screwing her eyes shut as tight as she can and not opening them, the drama queen again.

'Datty? Where Datty?' Pin's just not getting it.

'Weeeell, my child, we're not sure . . . exactly . . .'

Horatio looks hopelessly at the policeman, who hurriedly hands me the ivory-handled knife, which is stained with something, blood or rust, I don't know, can't tell, I'm shaking, going to faint.

'Wherever he is, he wanted you to have this.'

At the sight of it Scruff lets out an unearthly wail into the tall blue sky then wraps his arms around his head as if it'll shut everything off, make it all go away; Bert's just standing mute, in shock; Pin thumps me like I've just killed our father myself.

And somewhere from far, far away I'm hearing some kind of explanation: 'It's all up in the air . . . the Melbourne lot aren't too keen, an aunt just left . . . they're so very *Australian* . . . the blackfellas look out for them . . . the eldest kids are crack shots, real bushies, could kill a King Brown with a spade but cripes, not sure how they'd go in the big smoke . . .'

'Yee-ees.' Horatio's now inching back and looking around as if he expects monster crocs as well as deadly snakes to emerge from under house, dog and car any moment. He goes to say something – but another fly pops in his mouth. Miraculous.

'Well, blow me over with a feather,' the policeman says, and we're all now gazing in wonder at this exotically fabulous creature before us. A bona fide Fly Magnet no less. Priceless in these parts.

'Who *are* you?' Scruff asks to no one in particular.

'Species: lawyer,' the policeman helpfully explains. 'Habitat: Pall Mall, London. Food: pheasant, I'm guessing, from the looks of him, and treacle and, er . . .'

'Fly!' Horatio declares. 'I'm your human fly trap. Didn't you realise?'

'Can we keep him?' Pin squeals in excitement, clapping his hands.

What a perfect accessory out here. Suddenly, despite ourselves, we're all laughing. Mr Horatio swallows again then giggles as if he can't quite believe what he's just done. And at that I get the feeling that this bizarre person from another planet entirely could, actually, grow on us. Because he's got the air of someone who's completely hopeless around kids – but possibly, inside, is one himself. A very big one. Which was what Dad was like a lot, especially when he was making slingshots with the exact knife I'm now squeezing tight, so tight, because I'm thinking of his cackly glee as he whittled away with it; my knuckles are bone white as I clutch that knife with the string around the handle that he rebound so perfectly, on his last night with us . . .

Dad. I can't bear it. No one to stroke my cheek with his finger, I can feel it even now, no one to tuck me up at night, no one to tell me I'm all right since he's the only one who ever does that.

'Who's Basti?' Scruff pipes up. The mood snaps to attention.

'Er . . . ah . . . you don't know?'

Evasion. Hmm. Not good. Scruff's right to be curious. This situation's suddenly getting stranger by the minute. A spider of fear creeps up my back. Who's Horatio, let alone Basti? Dad never mentioned either. And what's this Kensington Reptilarium? Now that sounds vaguely familiar but I'm not sure why, like it's from some childhood story because every night we'd snuggle around Dad in his big high bed and I'm sure he spoke of that place but I can't remember details among all the yarns of pyramids and mosques and temples and jungles – how could I forget! My head's spinning. Too much in it. Too much to set right. I step forward, my hand on Bucket.

Horatio blusters, defensive, nodding at me. 'Why, *everyone* knows Basti, young lady.'

'We don't,' I say, calm. Too calm. Not young and not a lady.

'He's just . . . Basti. And how terribly fortunate you are!'

'And what's this Kensi Rep-il-air-y thing?' Scruff scowls a squint.

'Ah! The Kensington Reptilarium is only *the* most magical, mysterious building in the whole of England –'

'England!' we all yell.

'Why, yes.' Horatio looks at us like we're quite mad. 'Where else do you think it would be?'

'Alice Springs?' Bert suggests, looking sideways, eyes narrowing, trying to take all this in. Because that's the farthest we've ever been, three hours east as the crow flies, population 950 and a mighty metropolis in our book.

'Oh no, good grief, the Reptilarium is in *London*. It's your new home. And believe me, you are the luckiest children in the whole wide world.'

'No we're not.' My voice is low, quiet. Because I absolutely love an adventure, dream of gulping up the world but on my own terms, no one else's, thank you very much. Accompanied by someone I can trust. And not abandoning my former world just like that.

'You're extremely poor now, you know,' Horatio chatters on. 'There's no money. Oh no. Not a jot. No one to run the land, pay bills, mend fences, er, feed animals.' He looks down at Bucket. My mouth goes dry. 'You're paupers, the lot of you. There's no other way to put it.'

The four of us silently back away, dreading what's coming next. I know Dad was endlessly having money problems but I can't believe it's come to this.

'You're to travel to England immediately. The bank's taking over the property. It has to. Do you understand?'

I do. I'm just not going to admit it, Mister Fancy Pants. Tears are coming again and I'm trying to hold them back. This is so . . . unfair. To lose *everything*, all at once. I look at my brothers and sister, they look back at me, as if I can make it better because I'm always doing that. Well, I can't, troops, I can't. But they're not hearing it.

'There's not a second to be wasted,' Horatio urges. 'I represent Basti. I'm here to collect you.' Four faces stare up at him, stock-still, not budging an inch. 'The alternative is an orphanage. It can be arranged, you know.'

The policeman nods, grim. Like there's no escape

from this. Bushy to bushy there's just nothing he can do, sorry mates.

I gulp. An orphanage. One of those places with flour sacks for blankets and whippings and wallopings and walls so high you can never, ever escape. Maybe we shouldn't have been so . . . boisterous . . . with Aunty Ethel. Maybe she was our best bet.

I've got to keep us together, keep us buoyant, keep us strong. Pin climbs onto my shoulders and hangs on tight and Scruff bolts his hand into my pocket and Bert wraps her fist around my waist and locks on fierce. Bert, of all people!

Nup, not budging. Any of us. All four of us silent and defiant before this city slicker, interlocked. Get the picture? Horatio just stands before us muttering, 'Reptilarium – orphanage, Reptilarium – orphanage,' as if he really can't decide.

'Leave this?' Scruff explodes. 'Our whole *life*? Our mum's buried under that desert rose over there, did you know?'

'She needs us!' Bert wails.

'Leave *Bucket*?' I hug our dingo girl tight.

'I'm afraid so, yes, all of it. Terribly sorry. A frightful mess . . .'

The policeman nods again, straight at me, pleading for help. Throws up his hands. I look around, bite my lip. Leave everything we fiercely love for that faraway place where the sky is so low it almost touches the rooftops and its bridge is falling down – we've heard all the stories, I've read all the books, Dickens and J.M. Barrie and Sherlock Holmes and my favourite, the history tales, *London Stories* – but now its eggs come in powder and ham in tins and the huns have just smashed it to smithereens, haven't they? And, and, what's left of it? Really. Anything? Roofs? Umbrellas? Spoons? Because hasn't everything been melted down?

Nope. We're not shifting. We can do this ourselves. Bert stomps over to her trusty bike with a snake basket on the handlebars that she's painted a fetching shade of black. Tyres long gone but she can get the steel rims to work. She hauls it up. Sits. Her face says it all: she's never shifting *in her life*, thank you very much.

'Now, who else has flying goggles besides Miss Kick?' Horatio enquires. 'Uncle Basti's plane is waiting most impatiently at the Alice Springs airfield. Did I mention that, Miss Albertina? Red leather seats. Customised. Just for him. Anti-aircraft guns still attached. Real pounders. Boom, boom.' He looks straight at Scruff, who's listening with his head cocked, and raises one eyebrow. 'Basti's fabulously wealthy, you know. We'll be island-hopping . . . Borneo, Sumatra, Ceylon, something like that, hopeless at geography, hopeless at quite a lot actually. But it's all those exotic places your madcap father has spent years visiting. Bunty the pilot, he'll know. I must say, chaps, the adventure of your life awaits . . .'

Scruff lets go of me. I know him: it's the guns, it's Dad's old haunts, a killer combo, he's on alert.

Bert cocks her head. Narrows her eyes. Looks suspiciously at this Horatio bloke. He nods.

'There'll be new outfits awaiting you in London, Albertina. Velvets, laces, collars and cuffs, all the fashions from Harrods. Paris, if you must!' He winks. Does this little hop and step sideways with arms outstretched. 'Brrrrmm.'

Right. Quite a dance he's got going there.

'Brrrrrrrrmmmmmmmmmmmm.'

Bert looks at him with her fists on her hips and her chin jutting out. Assessing. Horatio's plane does a little circle in the dirt and the brrmming gets louder. 'London, Paris, Harrods, Claridges, Selfridges! Fabric shops, to make your own fabulousness!' he chants then leaps onto the balcony and jumps off, clearing all five stairs at once.

That's it.

Bert jumps up and runs as fast as she can to the house with her hands wide, squealing: 'Goggles! Flying goggles! Bucket, quick. Daddy might be waiting for us at the other end!'

Bucket runs wildly after the Caddy in the family who's wanted to be a fashion designer in a world capital – any, take your pick – ever since she could walk. Yep, that'd be right: Horatio's managed to pick the one and only thing guaranteed to work with that girl. How did he know?

He looks straight at me. 'We'll be flying over the exact spot Miss Earhart is rumoured to have disappeared from. Can even stop on a nearby island if you'd like.'

I gasp. Number One hero: Amelia Earhart. I can just see it now . . . finding her, sunburnt and stricken but alive. The world acclaim. A new mum in my life and a pilot's apprentice to boot, all from sitting tall and squealy on those red leather seats with binoculars glued over the rumoured spot . . .

Bucket's now barking crazily with excitement. The policeman throws wide his hands like he's given up. He looks straight at me. 'Best dog in the desert, right? Leave her with me. She'll be waiting for you.'

'Yaaaaaaaaaaaaaaaaaaaaay!' Bert screams in joy. London, Paris, crowns and couture, here she comes.

And what can the rest of us do?

Nothing, I'm afraid, but fall into line.

Because it all seems to have been decided upon.

So. There we have it. London, Uncle Basti, the Kensington Reptilarium and goodness knows what else – here we come. The four of us, the whole fierce crazy lot.

Whether you like it or not.

4
THIS IS
NOT GOOD

What's in our eyes, usually?

By day: a world very flat, with a shimmery haze of heat resting on the horizon. Above it, an endless, hurting blue. Ripples of sand dunes the colour of rust, tracks of roos and rock wallabies and snakes. Spinifex tumbling, muddy waterholes, ghost gums like shinbones. By night: an enormous canopy of stars above us, like the most wondrous of circus tents. We've never seen two houses stuck together. Never seen buildings taller than the ground floor. Never seen a city in our lives.

And now this.

Grey, grey, relentless grey, and a bit of black. A gaggle of chimneys being furiously used. Cold like shock. Traffic that barely moves. The taste of it. Pale faces, so many, close, bunkered down into scarves, hats, coats. Rows of tall houses that look the same, then the piles of rubble, the sombre gaps. Bomb hits. Again and again, and more frequently as we get further into the city, closer to tube stations, to areas where the crowds are thickest. What's underneath these tangles of rubble? What did these people go through? We were so removed, from everything, in our desert place at the bottom of the world.

And then we stop.

Er, this is the Kensington Reptilarium? That most legendary place? Excuse me?

Because what's looming in front of us is the saddest-looking building we've ever seen in our lives. We were expecting turrets, ballrooms, stables and maids; servants lining up to greet us with trays of hot chocolate. Oh yes, we'd taken bets. But now this. A towering, six-storey house that gives nothing away except a curmudgeonly wish to be left utterly alone. Paint peels from the walls like giant sunburn, dead vines spill from neglected windowboxes, long smears of dirt run down the façade like the grubbiest of tear-streaked faces, rogue sproutings of grass emerge triumphant from cracked marble steps and a high mound of leaves laps at the door. The entire building has one thing written all over it: 'GO AWAY I DON'T LIKE YOU.'

'We're he-ere!' Horatio exclaims, like this dingy old dump is made up entirely of chocolate and marzipan.

'Don't tell me. Our new home.' Scruff's not impressed either.

'Indeed, young sir. The most magical building in the whole of England.'

Oh, I can just picture inside. Big sagging ceilings like cows' bellies, thick cobwebs for curtains, dust-covered, rotting bedclothes, bathroom tiles hosting unknown slime and a damp kind of cold that curls up in your bones like mould and can never be scraped out.

Scruff's gripping the car seat, Pin's trying to climb into his lap, Bert's picking the last of the paint off her nails as if she hasn't seen the house, and on top of it all it's starting to rain. Great. How very London. Welcome to our new world.

Horatio's having none of it. He flings the car door wide. 'Chop chop, chaps!'

'Aren't you coming with us?'

He glances at the house.

'Er, do you want me to? You don't need me now, surely. Do you?' He's suddenly blustery and agitated, checking his watch, glancing down the street. 'I really have so much . . . to do . . . we're running very late, you know. Very, very late.'

'But who's going to introduce us?'

'Why, your good selves. Possibly? Think of it as a little test, my dears, your first step towards London independence. The spirit of the Blitz, heading forth into unknown climes! Yes? No? It's wonderfully exciting and adventurous. Isn't it?' He looks at us helplessly. 'You're from the bush, aren't you? Self-sufficient, big, brave, tough, all that?'

'Do you *really* work for Basti?' I snap, dreams dissolving before our eyes.

'I – why – I – of course.' He looks again at his watch. 'It's just . . . er . . . I have a luncheon appointment at Claridges, right this instant, and if I'm not there immediately I may lose the hand of the woman who's to be the future Mrs Smythe-Hippet. I'm *thirty-nine*, girl. Don't you know what this means? Yes, I am pathetic, but have mercy upon my soul and GET OUT of the car. Please. The lot of you. Right now.'

I glare suspiciously. At the house, at Horatio. He was hopeless all the way over, toddling off to the closest club or bar wherever he could find one, telling us to 'play in the dirt, or whatever it is children do,' alerting me that we'd possibly flown over Amelia

Earhart's island the day before and it had slipped his mind to let me know, worse luck, old girl.

Scruff looks at my face then back at our chaperone. He stares at Horatio with his enormous doe eyes that fool everyone but his family – everyone melts at the sight of them but us.

'Dad won't like this,' he says. Dead quiet.

'What? You're warriors who wrestle snakes for breakfast and crush scorpions in your fist! I have been forewarned, you know. They make you tough out there – don't they?' Horatio pinches Scruff on his cheek, Pin shoots off Scruff's lap and the chauffeur revs as if he can't wait to get away from this wretched place.

The rain hardens. Horatio's now trying to haul Bert out but she's got an iron grip on Scruff. 'Don't you understand what it's like to be hopelessly in love? With a woman who insists on promptness at every moment and didn't want you gallivanting off to Australia in the first place? Do any of you understand this? Can you imagine what it's like to be desperate to see your beloved, no matter what?' He is suddenly very still. 'Can you?' he pleads, quite hopeless. 'Have you *ever* been in love?'

Bert looks at him as if it's just clicked. Nods, solemnly. Steps swiftly, obediently, into the pouring rain. 'I have, Horatio. Kick has no idea. She doesn't love anything because she's as mean and tough as old nails. *Especially* with her family. Of course we can do this by ourselves. Off you go, quick. My sister's just a big old bossy boots who doesn't care about us in any way – but I do. I've got a heart, unlike some.'

Right. I just want to kick her right there and then. Want to drive off in the car and leave her here all by herself. This is punishment, of course, for me telling her endlessly on the way over that no, we can't make a diversion to find some purple Thai silk and no, we can't let Scruff fire the guns for target practice. 'You're not my father! You're not my mother! So stop telling us what to *do*,' was the constant refrain, rat-tat-tatting into me.

Bert pokes out her tongue at me now, in triumph, then turns to our dubious new home. Which we will soon be entering all by ourselves, thanks to her impetuousness and stubbornness and unending desire to do the opposite of whatever I want. 'There's family inside, isn't there, Horatio?' she continues solemnly. 'Maybe Daddy's here. *Some* of us actually care about that.' She glares daggers at me. 'Come on, troops. Christmas is close. We've got work to do.'

I sigh. She's delusional about Dad and now's not the place to enlighten her. Horatio's just biting his lip: he's no use. I want a bit of certainty, for once; want to know this is a situation we can trust. Want to stay in the warmth of this car, to end up anywhere but this wreck of a place, but Bert's said the magic words no matter how impossible they are – *Dad might be in there* – and suddenly the rest of them are right beside her on the pavement, looking hopefully at their determined new boss who's just supplanted the eldest Caddy of the group.

'Datty.' Pin looks to the house, trustingly.

I shut my eyes. It's beyond horrible.

Horatio murmurs, 'Bless you, my children, our future is assured,' and departs quick smart as if he can't wait to get away from the place. 'Knock nice and loud,' he flusters then slams his car door and winds down the window. 'Basti will be home, he's always home, he never goes anywhere.'

Bert goes to ask something – as if she's only just realised what she's got us all in for – but 'The knocker, the knocker!' Horatio urges over the top of her as his car pulls away gratefully. 'Muscles, Master Scruff!' he mimes, pounding on the door. 'It's what won the war, eh? And proper clothes, young lady.' He stares at me as if it's only just dawned on him that I may not have the right look for a grand London establishment. 'For God's sake, a *dress*.'

I bristle, thanks mate; want to kick him now too.

'The attic. Something red. It's your colour, young lady, believe it or not.' He laughs as if he's just told an enormous joke. 'Yes. Quite terrifying.'

'What? Me, or the house?' I yell, throwing my coolie hat at the departing car.

The sky's the colour of a battleship and the cold . . . I groan. It's brutal, and we're woefully unprepared for it. We're used to heat that fries eggs on a car bonnet and guess what? We're dressed in a crazy collection of army shorts and string vests and sarongs and military jackets that were found anywhere and everywhere along the way. By yours truly. Every morning, before I'd attempt to wake Horatio up, because he always overslept. To get him to England, quick smart, to a country that may just understand what Christmas is all about before Christmas has been and gone and we miss it entirely this year. And of course we'd forgotten to pack anything remotely useful in the mad rush to those delicious-sounding red seats. All I managed was Dad's old knife with the string around the handle plus my slingshot and Dad's copy of *The Jungle Book*.

Horatio only realised the dire clothing situation somewhere above Ceylon and shouted a thrillingly banned word (promptly recorded by Scruff in his spy notebook) and now it's suddenly midwinter and there's not a single overcoat among us; Scruff doesn't even have shoes. And we're terrifyingly alone. Horatio's left us with no forwarding address, no contact details of any kind. So. Great. Dumped, in the middle of a London street. In front of a wreck that doesn't look like anyone's lived in it for a hundred years. We usually love being alone, love a place all to ourselves; as long as we know a parent and love and jolliness and warmth is still somehow attached to it. But this?

The blackest, widest, dustiest front door you've ever seen looms before us. It's covered in cobwebs. Leaves are banked up to our knees. Bert's blinking away tears because she's suddenly cottoned on: no, of course, Daddy couldn't possibly be in this. It's a trick. She's extremely good at pretending she's so very grown-up; the last thing she wants is for people to think she's as soft as a pocket, but she's reached her limit right now, I just know. I put my hand on her shoulder.

She shrugs it away. 'I hate you. I don't need you. I never do. You're not my mother. Leave me alone.'

I bite my lip.

'The knocker,' Scruff urges in exactly Horatio's voice, poking me in the back. 'Come on, Kick. Quick.'

Thanks, mate. It's coming from all quarters here. The door doesn't look welcoming in any way and why *was* Horatio so afraid of it? I look up the street: the car's well and truly gone. No help anywhere. Has to be done. 'Damn, damn, *double DAMN*.'

'Dan! Dan!' Pin claps wildly with excitement at yet another thrillingly forbidden word. From his big sister no less, the one who's always scooping out yummy ants from his mouth and saying 'no' in a cranky voice.

'Damn,' Scruff corrects drily from a distance. 'And courtesy of Miss Bossy Boots, of all people.' He cackles with glee.

'*Naughty* Kicky.' Pin wags his finger. 'No, no no.' Oh, he's loving that. Scruff's now throwing his finger in there, wagging it wildly – Bert joins in too. 'Damn, damn,' Pin taunts.

We're all laughing now, can't help it, and suddenly I'm punching my arms in the air and declaring, 'It's going to be okay, you crazy crazies. We'll make this work! Anything you want, fire away, come on.'

'I'm hungry,' Pin wails, seizing the opening.

I groan. Of course. Food. The other thing that's not gone to plan. We're starving, the lot of us. Yet I can't quite bring myself to approach that terrifying door; it's a feeling in the pit of my stomach.

Meanwhile Scruff is now balancing a dead spider on his finger and lecturing it in exactly Horatio's voice: 'Now don't you go expecting anything like a Christmas here, young chap. There'll be no pudding, oh no, not so much as a ginger snap. Got it? You're from the bush, remember. Tough. Eh, what?'

'I want Christmas,' Pin wails.

My fists are clenched. One thing at a time, troops. And Christmas, of course, is just a few sodding days away. Feeling positively ill now.

The light's feeble like it hasn't had enough vegetables. A rubbly hole is all that's left of the house next door and a naked doll with dead eyes stares from a puddle and it's as close to a present that Bert's going to get in this place, I can feel it in my bones, and she hates dolls. A dead rat's in the gutter with its horribly sharp teeth bared – urgh – and the garden square across the street has tall, black trees with enormous witches' hands clawing at the sky and that'll keep Pin awake, every night, clutched to my neck, I just know it.

'Hey, look at the garden fence,' I exclaim cheerily, trying to distract them from a missing dad, home, dog, Christmas; trying to distract them from entering a terrifying new life just yet. 'The railings have disappeared. It's just the posts. I wonder what happened.'

'I stole them for my master's cages to put the delicious new little kiddies in,' Scruff says in his Horatio voice that I want to throttle now. 'Mmmm, all that lovely new flesh.' He smacks his lips.

Bert just looks at him witheringly – this is a girl, after all, who wants to dig up dead people out of curiosity.

'The war took them. In case you're wondering. Which you obviously are.'

We nearly jump out of our skins. Turn. To a woman who has appeared behind us. Silently, as if by magic. With black hair and red lips and the palest skin and an umbrella that looks like it's made out of zebra hide and a fur coat so fabulously ivory-black I can smell Bert's envy; she wants to crawl right inside it and curl up. In fact, yep, there she is, stroking its softness with adoration, she can't help it.

I yank her back.

'The war took away our very smart fence and I did love it so,' the woman says, enfolding Bert firmly into her coat as if she's trying to steal her in broad daylight. 'It melted down the railings and turned them into tanks, just like that.' She whoops with laughter as if Bert's just found her secret giggle-spot. 'They haven't quite come back yet but they will, oh they will. Some day.' Then she looks intently at all of

47

us, up and down. 'I say, are you lost? Is there a fancy dress party I haven't been invited to? I do hope not.'

I glance back at the Reptilarium, speechless. Don't know if we're lost, can't explain; what's happened to my brain? This is ridiculous. Apparently there's an uncle but we don't want to go inside. Haven't tried, should, yes, of course, but something's stopping us, not sure what. A feeling, just that, a sense of unwelcomeness . . .

Bert's now hugging one of the lady's legs and pouring every ounce of love into her in an intensely passionate and dark Bert-way.

The woman hovers her hand over Bert's thin little back as if she's not quite sure what to do, to dare, next. 'Are you looking for someone? Can I be of assistance perhaps?'

The voice is suddenly low and motherly and it's been so long since anything like that, for any of us. Mum's voice is what I remember the most, her voice saying my name, and her fingertips soft on my earlobe and her hoot of a laugh. Bert hugs tighter, it's got her too. There's a soft gulp of a cry-about-to-start; it'll be floods in a moment.

'We need Uncle Basti,' Scruff pipes up.

'Basti?' The woman steps back in horror. Looks at us afresh. 'You're attached to *him*?'

Glances at his house then back at us, as if we're infected.

'Right. Well, I better leave you then. Off you go, toodle pip.' And she indicates the big black door. Bert's briskly ejected from leg and coat. 'Good luck,' she murmurs. 'You'll need it, must dash.' She disappears fast into the house on the other side of the Reptilarium without a backward glance.

Gosh.

Gone.

Completely, utterly. I tug my earlobe in bewilderment.

Bert cries, anguished, 'Wait!', but the door's firmly shut.

Leaving us completely alone, all over again.

Right. Well, there you go. Scruff grabs the closest thing – Pin's beloved teddy, Banjo – and hurls him in frustration across the street. We all gasp in shock. Bert wails, punches him. Scruff opens his mouth to the heavens and Pin bawls then bites his brother hard – he's absolutely forbidden to do this, Dad'd be marching him off to the chook house at this point and shutting him up in it – and me? Absolutely no idea what to do except sob right here in the street. For Dad, for Horatio, for help, for anything to get us out of this mess.

But can't.

I shut my eyes and squeeze my hands over my ears, just shut it all out. Want to be somewhere, anywhere, still and quiet and alone. Blissfully alone, just reading a book, the thing I love more than anything in the world because when I'm doing that it's like I calm down into stillness, I uncurl into someone else entirely, someone who I actually like and want to be with in a world that actually works. Is on my side. But this is just horrible, horrible, horrible and they're all expecting me to get them out of it. Can't. Just . . . can't.

'Look,' Scruff whispers, tugging my sleeve. I shrug him off, savagely, don't want to know. 'No, Kicky, *look*.'

'What?'

I look up. Bert's mouth is wide open. Pin's giggling and pointing around her in delight.

'All the houses.'

Oh. My. Goodness.

Because as the light drops, all the windows of the houses in the square are aglow, with a warm and buttery softness. As if a whole new world is suddenly, magically, coming alive; turning into something else. With a great swelling of loveliness and care and concern; a feast of food and toasty beds to sink in and Christmas trees and gifts and goodness knows what else.

A smile of resolve blazes through me. I need all this for my lot. We've come this far, they deserve it, and by jingo I'm going to get it for them. Because from the Reptilarium, also, is a whisper of a glow like the faint pulse of a heartbeat, barely alive. But *there*.

'Troops, action stations!' I command.

Swiftly before me, in a sudden line, is a row of three perfect salutes. I grab all the hands I can get. 'Family, here we come. We can do this – we're from the bush! Boy Hero, you ready?'

'As I'll ever be,' Scruff whispers.

'Girl Hero?'

She actually squeals. Most uncharacteristically Bert.

'Captain?'

'Aye aye,' Pin giggles, and throws in another salute.

I march us forward. Great excitement. Clang the lion's mouth. We're here! We've arrived! We're staaaaaaaarving!

No answer.

'Uncle Basti,' I yell.

No answer still.

'Helloooooooooo!'

We wait, and wait.

'Hello?'

An enormous, spooky silence.

This *can't* be happening. Horatio said Basti never goes out. I step back. Stare at the square.

Surrounding us, as the afternoon light softens completely away, are real Christmas trees, paper snowflakes and little presents in the glowing windows of every single house – except this one. Oh, it's all handmade – paper and silver fabric and kids' cutouts – but everything is so sparkly and magical and alive, with love and delight and celebration and warmth. It feels like we've landed in the middle of a neighbourhood that's busily, joyously, making do, with gratitude and giggles, after years of austerity and sacrifice and going-without. It feels so welcoming. Caring. Fun.

The exact opposite of the scruffy meanness of this house upon whose doorstep we've been dumped. I shiver. Feel sick again. This is some cruel joke. I look at Scruff.

'Maybe we should get adopted,' he says.

I shut my eyes tight. The rain's getting harder, it's hurting now, we *have* to get inside; deep breath, doorknob's grabbed and as I go to push it with all my might, miraculously, at that very moment, the door glides silently, spookily, ominously open. Just like that.

We look at each other. Scruff nods, urging me in first. That'd be right. Bert pushes me with one, clinching word. 'Daddy.'

'Daddy,' the rest of them whisper.

I step inside. The others are close behind.

Gasps, from all of us.

5
DEATH
MAY FOLLOW

It's not a house at all.

Well, the first little bit of it is. The entrance hall, which looks very much like what an entrance should look like, with a hat rack and an umbrella stand and a mirror. But then there's a door. Quite a modest little thing. Which of course we open, because why not? We're from the bush and haven't been raised along those lines of 'children should be seen and not heard' and all that, 'children should just wait, patiently wait, in endless, non-fidgety stillness' etc., etc. – oh no, we can't possibly do any of that.

We push this door wide . . . and that's when more gasps come in.

Before us: an enormous tower. As if we're suddenly inside a lighthouse. But in the middle of a city. In what appears to be an extremely scruffy but utterly normal house – but it's not. Wondrously. And from floor to ceiling are what look like cages. Containing, well, we can't make out exactly what in the low honey light from hundreds of candles, all around us, right up to the sky. Someone likes their candles a lot here and I smile because I do too, much more than the harshness of electricity, as did Mum; the flickering softness of their lovely light.

The door shuts firmly behind us. We jump. Locked. Can't get out.

Goosebumps.

Pin's fingers find mine, the candles shiver as if from an invisible breath, the hairs rise on the back of my neck. We're being watched. I just know it. We spin around.

'Hello?' I try saying but nothing comes out.

Heart's pounding. Mustn't let them know. Must be in control of this. The candles catch the gold in the tiles at our feet and the brass bars of the cages that reach up to a glittery golden dome high above us. It's an enormous star with five plunging points and through huge slivers of glass is the London sky with its rain silently streaking, like enormous, fat tears.

It's the most beautiful thing I've ever seen and the saddest, all at once, like this whole place is crying.

Boom! The centre of the room bursts into a blinding white light. As if a war spotlight's been switched on.

'W-what's that?' Scruff grabs my arm. Points.

An enormous cage on a circular mahogany table. Dead centre.

A brass plaque resting in front of it.

ENTER AT OWN RISK
DEATH MAY FOLLOW

Right. That's saying it. Blood, pounding in my ears. Hands, trembling. And yep, this is the toughest girl in the desert here. The one who chases roos with woomeras and decapitates venomous snakes in a single blow, who tames dingos and rides emus and who always sets things right.

'Kick?' Bert urges. 'Come on.'

Teeth, clenched. Reputation must be maintained. I step firmly towards the cage – and reel back. Because inside, staring with cool yellow eyes as knowing as a cat's, is a cobra. Coil upon coil. In front of it is an extremely dead mouse on its back, red eyes wide in shock. And the clasp that holds the cage shut is just a tiny, breakable slither of a thread.

'Kick, i-isn't that one of the deadliest snakes in the world?' Scruff whispers.

Can't speak.

'I'll take that as a yes.'

Out flicks the snake's tongue, tasting the new scent of very young – very fresh – flesh. That would be ours. Slowly I retreat, hands pulling Bert and Pin with me, soothing, 'Sssshhhhhhh.'

'Daddeeeeeeeeee!' Pin suddenly wails, losing his nerve.

That's it. It's all on. Pin screaming, Bert jumping up and down and giggling – 'New toy! This is more like it! None of that doll stuff!' – and Scruff murmuring, terrified, 'Nice snaky, nice snaky, she'll be right.'

'Can anyone help – I mean, hear?' I yell loudly to the waiting house.

We spin around. In the long silence that follows are rustling and hissing, clicking and scrabbling noises. As if the place itself is alive, the very air of it. As if we're deep in the Amazonian jungle and it feels like there are whispers over the animal sounds, we can almost make words out and turn in a mystified, horrified huddle. Because it feels like hundreds of eyes – thousands of them – from all manner of invisible creatures from around the building are looking straight at us. Checking us out. And licking their lips.

How to get out? Get a rescue happening here? Make us all safe? I look wildly around. There are wooden ladders on brass railings up to the ceiling and on various levels are doors leading off to goodness knows what. Need to move, think, fast, or Pin's going to be swallowed up by fright and Bert's going to let that cobra out. Scruff's just standing behind me making a terrified humming noise and it's getting louder and louder and the cobra's now banging angrily against its cage; it wants the sound shut off as much as I do and it's only a tiny thread holding it in, mate.

'Scruuuuuuuuuuuuff!' I cry.

He jerks still.

'I'm, I'm going –'

'Where, Kick, where?' He looks up at the cages in terror.

'I don't know,' I cry.

Bert stamps her foot crossly, exasperated – 'You two' – and heads straight to a ladder.

It snaps me to attention. 'I'm first, missy miss.'

'Why you?' Bert snaps. 'Are you leaving us down here by ourselves to get killed, perhaps? That'd be right. Miss Bossy Boots, the champion of bossy boots.'

Pin wails.

'Whatever's up there, I'll be harder to swallow, all right? Listen. Stay right behind me. The lot of you.'

Bert sticks out her tongue at me then at the cobra. The snake responds with another cool flick of its tongue as if to say, yes, little minx, we'll see about that, I'll tell you who's boss.

There's a sudden, piercing whistle from above. We jump. Gaze skyward.

Hurtling down from the ceiling is a huge hook on a brass chain. Speared on it, a piece of old parchment. It stops at eye-level. Jiggles. I step back. It jiggles more urgently.

'I think it likes you,' Scruff says.

It jiggles again as if in approval. I extract the paper from the hook.

It's an ad. An extremely old one . . .

THE KENSINGTON
REPTILARIUM

Snakes! Deadly and otherwise.
Slowworms!
Glowworms!
Lizards! Chameleons!
Land and water tortoises, etc.!
In great variety
from all parts of the globe . . .

ENTER
IF YOU DARE

Bert exclaims ecstatically at the announcement of each new creature – she can't wait to go exploring. Pushes me impatiently. I start climbing the nearest ladder, accompanied by an enormous swelling of clicking and scrabbling and hissing sounds; on and on, Bert jumpy with impatience behind me. The first-floor platform. Now eye to eye with snakes and chameleons and . . . rats. Yep. Rats. Hate them. It's just a thing I have.

I grip the ladder tighter, break out in a sweat, can't go on, can't climb higher, this is horrible. Bert pokes me sharply. Ow! No choice. On I go. The creatures are from all over the world; some I recognise from Australia, some from Alice. *Home.* My mouth goes dry. This is too mysterious. Why are we here? Really. Did Dad know about all this? How are we connected with this place? Everyone's bunching up the ladder behind me. I climb across to another ladder and *whiiiiiiiiiiiiiiiiiiiz!*

Goodness. Gobsmacked. Because I've just zoomed across the room. At astonishing speed.

It's like a secret button's been activated. In a flash we're jumping on new ladders, sliding across brass railings to other parts of the building and gliding to smooth exact stops right by ladders waiting patiently to take us to another level, and another, higher and higher. Right up to the glass roof, we can almost touch it and the place is now ringing with our glee. It's ingenious! Amazing! Someone's had an awful lot of giggles designing this, someone who knows a lot about kids . . .

'I'm staying here foreveeeeeeeeeeeeeeer!' Scruff sings as he flies across the room, stopping now and then to announce the occupant of another cage, and another, from their little brass plaques attached to the bars.

'Taipan – Deadliest Snake in the World. Well, *hello*, little boy . . . Goat-Eating Serpent. My, how pretty you are . . . Bearded Dragon. Show me your necklace. Come on . . . Man-eating Python. Not the Scruffter, lovely. My sisters, yes . . . Tiger spider. Death in three minutes. How about two? . . . King Brown – Second Deadliest Snake in the World. Woohoo, this boy's from home!' Scruff stops. 'But . . . hang on. Only Daddy's ever caught one alive . . . he's world-famous for it. We have the newspaper story – how did this one . . .?'

I shake my head, bewildered. It's all too mysterious. The low sky's right above me, I put up both palms, touch the raindrop tears through the glass, they fall and fall.

Hang on –

A sound –

'Ssssh!'

Is it possible to hear through your skin . . . with your whole being . . . with *goosebumps*? It's a strange, soothing singing wrapped up like a cocoon of loveliness within the very core of the reptilian noise, like a lullaby inside a shell inside an ocean's inky depths. It makes me feel very safe. I just want to curl up inside it and close my eyes, and sleep.

'I hear it too,' Scruff whispers in wonder.

'Mama,' Pin cries. He's never said that in his life; my heart snags.

Bert moves across, cuddles him fiercely. 'It's okay, little man, it's all right. Where's it coming from, troops?'

'There.' Pin points. At a beautifully carved door two floors down, smaller than the rest, with swirling snakes and lizards picked out in paint. I whistle low – it's the hunting signal used to track roos; we're going in.

We glide like swans to the door from our different ladders. Four sets of ears press to the wood. Yep, Pin's right, the sound's inside. I knock gently. The singing stops. Bert thumps loudly, can't help herself, still refusing to believe – 'Daddy! Basti!'

I wince.

'Should we just open it?' Scruff whispers.

I nod. Reluctantly. The singing sounds so private and personal, it's not for us. But Bert's had enough, there's too much at stake here, she flings open the door . . .

'Golly galoshes,' she whispers. The last time she said that was when a willy-willy tore our water tower clean into the sky.

6

PLEASE MAY I INTRODUCE...

We've never seen anything like it.

The most deliciously comfortable-looking hidey hole; toasty warm with a huge red velvet couch piled high with cushions and blankets and furs, enormous armchairs on lion rugs complete with heads attached, tables stacked with books, wonderful books, so many – I can't wait! – and a roaring fire happily spitting and cracking, a huge stuffed polar bear wearing a top hat in a corner upon whose arms are resting an assortment of umbrellas, and on the wood-panelled walls are paintings, in every available space, tall, tiny, oval, right up to the roof; all portraits, men, women and children, with one thing in common – startling eyes, one green, one blue.

Five other people have those eyes. The four of us here. And Dad.

'Well, hello, hello,' I smile. '*This* is more like it.'

It feels like we're being pulled inside by something stronger than us, an invisible thread, luring us further and further into this enchanting space and we want to gaze at, devour, every person in the portraits, sink into the chairs, sleep, yet the room feels so private . . .

We haven't been invited . . . but is someone . . . *here*?

My breathing's wobbly, I've suddenly never felt so wrong and rude and intrusive in my life and, as the four of us creep inside, the strangest thing happens: the reptilian cacophony behind us hushes, as if every single creature in the building is now straining its ears, listening in and wondering what's going to happen next. What we'll dare.

Pin's now tight in my arms. Scruff's got Bert sternly by the hand. The singing has been accompanying a gramophone in the corner – as if its owner needs to drown the very thought of us out. The voice now departs from the music and drops to a rapid, soothing chatter. I can't make anything out.

'Hello!' Pin sings out loud, excited, oblivious.

The chattering stops abruptly.

Breaths held. Then up comes – slowly, slowly – an old, green, leather flying hat. Trembling. As though it really doesn't want to be emerging at all. On top of a flurry of hair as red and unbrushed as our own. Above some round silver glasses with lenses as shiny as mirrors. We lean in, peer. The glasses flip up with a snap. We gasp.

For staring at us is a pair of eyes: one blue, one green. But they're not in any way thrilled to be seeing long-lost relatives from across the world, oh no. They're horrified. So appalled and disgusted, in fact, that the head they belong to is refusing to rise a single inch more. What a sight we must be, the whole raggedy, grubby lot of us. Not London at all, no, Horatio, you were right.

It's enough for Bert. She leaps at the hat and enfolds the face it belongs to in a ferocious cuddle of love using every ounce of her parentless strength.

Pin cries, 'Mama! Dada!'

'Will you adopt us?' Scruff demands.

The eyebrows arch wildly in shock and arms encased in blue velvet struggle for balance, a muffled cry coming from somewhere within it all. But it's smothered by Bert's fervour, Scruff's glee, Pin's straining for this exciting new creature who's the key to everything being repaired and happy and fixed in our lives. It's my signal. Sorry. Can't help it. Family's the one thing this lot needs at this point.

I hold out my hand for a shaking, tugging Bert back
with the other.

But nothing.

Just my fingers hovering, embarrassed, in empty
air. I move closer, urging them to be grasped.
They're being examined like they're riddled with
pox. I tremble. I'm not going to cry, I'm *not*. But . . .
my eyes prickle. I drop my hand. What's wrong
with it? Too grubby? Stinky from the bush? Not
girly enough? I suddenly feel completely, utterly,
horribly . . . unwelcome. What's a lady meant to
be like? Dirt's under my nails in little moons and
the cracks of my palms are like river lines on a map.
I wipe my hands furiously on my shorts and start all
over again, a smile stretched tight.

Nothing. Again.

What's *wrong* with me?

I stare despairingly at two eyes glaring with . . .
what? Hostility. Coldness. Horror. *No*. Ridiculous.
We're *family*.

I bite my lip. He's not going to see my furious
tears, he's not. I look around. Horatio, this was a
mistake. A humiliating one. We need to exit here.
Fast. Get to Claridges, the hotel where you've
headed to. Get a new family, a new house. I wipe
my eyes fiercely.

Scruff looks at me, ever the trusty lieutenant, wondering what's next, because of course I'm the big tough desert pirate who's always making things right for them – crow's nest lookouts and slippery-slide mattresses and flying foxes and cuddles and kisses goodnight. Yep, the queen of it, whether Bert likes it or not. But now this. And I'm stumped. Because we're utterly unwanted. It's as simple, and as horrible, as that.

A deep breath. I'll be bigger than him. I smile wider and hold out my hand once again. 'I'm Kick. Very pleased to meet you, Basti.'

Nothing.

Bert's had enough. She jumps on the sofa, plucks the flying cap off the new head with a gleeful cackle, clips it on her curls and balances on the back rim of the seat like a world-famous tightrope walker gathering up the adulation of the crowd, just as she does, endlessly, on the picket fence at home. Arches into a backflip. Then turns to the hostile eyes and holds her fists under her armpits like a monkey. No! No! An extremely cheeky monkey, which is precisely the most completely wrong thing at this point. And a monkey who's, er, proudly in possession of a brand new hat.

'Albertina!' Scruff and I shout in exactly Dad's voice. 'Are you mad? So sorry.'

We're apologising profusely to the new eyes but they're now focused on something else: our crazy brother on the end of the couch preparing for his very own death-defying circus routine, the running jump and flip, as if he wants to compete with Bert. Because someone's always there to catch him – us. But no one's there now. We're too far from him and there's no time. And just as he flips and propels himself wildly into the empty air the hat owner leaps forward – quick as a flash – and catches him in his arms. As if he knew all along the boy was going to do this.

'Wheeeeeeeeee!' Pin sings in gratitude. 'Basti the best,' he says, then turns his rescuer's cheeks insistently this way and that by firmly steering his chin – 'Turn around, turn around, now, other cheek' – as he plants big smacks of kisses on both sides of his uncle's face.

Basti drops him abruptly to the ground.

'Ow!'

Our uncle reels back in terror, checking his pockets, patting them, making sure everything is all right and in its place. As if he's never been kissed in his life, as if he's never seen a child, held one, as if he's just been infected with the most deadliest of germs and the interlopers are out to steal his valuables and pets and handkerchiefs and entire life.

'I do not *do CHILDREN*,' he roars.

Dead silence.

A chameleon suddenly appears from behind his shoulder. '*That* is why.' His eyes dart to his friend. 'I have too many other things to think about.' The creature runs up Basti's head, perches on the top, tilts its face and rapidly changes from blue to red. The four of us giggle, can't help it. It hisses angrily back.

Right. Great. So even the animals here feel the same way about us. A green tree-python peeks delicately out of one jacket pocket and a frill-necked lizard out of the other.

Scruff says 'good day' to each of them, can't help himself; Bert mouths the same. Python and lizard disappear fast into pocket depths. Our host's face is like thunder.

'Obviously you did not get the wire.'

Silence.

'I cannot possibly take you in. An orphanage in Berkshire awaits. All has been arranged. Mr Smythe-Hippet was meant to – *meant* to – deliver you there directly. This is a mistake.'

Four Caddy mouths, wide with horror.

'Speaking of, where *is* the man?'

'There was a lady he had to meet,' Bert pipes up. 'The future Mrs Smythe-Hippet. He's *thirty-nine*. It's dire. His life is almost over.'

Uncle Basti screws up his face in shock, in revulsion. 'I don't want to know. Because while he's gallivanting about town I'm stuck with you. Aren't I? Most unfortunately. This wasn't meant to happen. Charlie Boo – where are you?' Basti raises his voice in panic, but no one answers back. A horribly awkward silence. '*Where's* Charlie Boo when I need him? DON'T EVEN DARE TO GET COMFORTABLE.' He glares at little Pin, who's now sunk to the ground as if the weight of this trauma is just too much to bear. '*Don't* get comfortable, oh no. You'll only be here for five minutes, young man.'

We stare, stunned. This brother of our father is not like our father at all. In any way. Doesn't sound like him, doesn't look like him. No wonder he was never mentioned. They must have had some huge and horrible falling out.

Basti's wearing a battered red soldier's jacket with brass buttons from some war of long ago; black trousers with gold braid up the sides; one green sock, one yellow, and long black velvet slippers that have a B embroidered on them in thread as golden as egg yolk. He looks like he's from another world entirely, like he's missed – completely – the last six years of the war. And Dad – the polar opposite. All grizzly muscles and khaki and workboots and a stained bushman's hat that rarely comes off.

'I bet you were never even in a war!' I fling, can't help it, as I scoop Pin up, thinking of Turk bullets and trench whistles left back at home. Thinking of proper, grown-up, fighting men; out in the world, on secret expeditions, doing something with their lives.

Basti flips up his glasses, takes another close look at the sheer and utter stain of me, shivers in revulsion and what feels like a cold, cold hatred, and flips the glasses back.

'Ignore her, mate,' Scruff says companionably. 'She's just the embarrassing big sister going through . . . whatever girls go through.' It's his turn to shiver. 'Ask Aunty Ethel. She'll tell you. My sister's always rubbing people up the wrong way. Hey, you know, we wouldn't mind something to eat here. I bet you've got a corker of a kitchen. Down . . . there . . . is it? I love to cook. Eggs. My specialty.'

'What?' Basti hisses.

He steps forward, head to one side. Utterly bewildered by the astonishingly talky, grubby tidal wave of us. Peers at the freckles that cram everyone's faces as if he's never seen anything like them. Shudders. Peers at our eyes like he doesn't quite trust the colour of them, like we're impostors who couldn't possibly belong to this esteemed family that graces every inch of his precious velvety space.

'We'll be up on this wall one day!' Scruff jumps in cheerily, following his uncle's eyes and flinging his arms wide. 'Continuing the proud family tradition. Bags the centre spot! Just need some food first, or I might die sooner than expected.' He laughs. 'How about it, Uncle Basti. Any bananas in the house? Jam? Chocolate?'

'I don't. Think. So.' Basti peers at the embarrassment of our mishmash of clothes. The affront of Scruff's bare feet. The horror of our filthy faces still faintly marked by desert war paint. He's making us feel like nothing so much as a brand new species of reptile here – a species that's never going to pass muster. And on top of everything, a species that steals hats. He glares at his now.

Bert backs up, trembling. It's a splendid new fashion item – and we all know how much she'll be wanting to hang onto it.

'No cage, Uncle Basti,' she says nervously, holding her head. 'Please.'

'He's not going to put you in a cage,' I soothe, steely, staring straight at him.

'Unless you don't give that hat back, Albertina,' Scruff says, through gritted teeth.

Basti raises his eyebrows. An idea. Bert whips back the hat quick smart. It's clipped onto its rightful head.

'Chocolate's my favourite thing, Basti,' Scruff announces, man to man. 'I get violently ill if I don't have some every hour, on the hour.'

'Ssssh.' I kick him. Doesn't he get it? We're *not wanted*.

Scruff punches me hard, I punch back.

Basti backs away fast, holding up his hands. 'No. No. No. I don't do little people. Especially fighting ones. Absolutely not. This stops now.'

'We can be angels, too,' Bert jumps in eagerly. 'We'll even take your pets for walks.'

'Pets! Pets!' Pin cries excitedly. 'Bags Cobry!'

'Why *meeeee*?' Basti yells to the heavens.

'Because we don't have anyone else,' I yell back.

Everything, suddenly, is very still.

'I –' Basti stops. 'I don't . . . I just . . . can't . . .' His glasses snap back. 'I don't do *people*. Children. Especially.'

'Even tiny little ones?' Pin asks, his enormous eyes welling.

I find Pin's hand. It's shaking, I've never felt it shake before; I squeeze it, with all my heart, willing him not to cry. It's no use. A big plop of wet falls on my hand, which is then used to wipe his nose, noisily, leaving a streak of snivelly dirt across his cheek.

Basti stares, repulsed. 'I've heard things,' he says, backing away. '*Especially* about the desert variety of child. Oh yes, I know exactly what you're like. I have my ways. For instance, I know that *Childus Australis Desertus* has not only shoe phobias –' (glaring at Scruff's feet) '– and kleptomania, especially when it comes to clothes, which are then customised most bizarrely –' (Bert) '– but also turns every meal into a battlefield –' (wincing at Pin) '– and can never be still or contained or quiet –' (Scruff) '– and bangs on any available pot like they're creating an orchestral symphony –' (Pin again) '– and battles policemen and frankly anyone in authority –' (all of us) '– and is quite wilfully the opposite of whatever a lady is meant to be –' (me in particular) '– with the most terrifyingly hotheaded temper and is far too outspoken and loud and stroppy for their own good –' (definitely me) '– and is quite despairingly wild, stubborn, obnoxious, exhausting and disobedient –' (all of us) '– until your reputation has become so blighted that no one, absolutely no one, wants to go near you, I'm afraid. Especially, *most* especially . . . me.'

He takes a deep breath. 'So there you have it. I cannot help you. At all. I live in an extremely orderly house. An extremely orderly and deeply *secret* house that will be destroyed if it is ever discovered. And I just know in my bones that you all being here will draw attention to it. *Fatal* attention. Your noise, your shrillness, your fulsome . . . *bounce.* This place carries out some extremely important work with rare and exotic animals – and it cannot be disturbed under any circumstances. I haven't ventured outside for years. I need to protect what goes on here. So, frightfully sorry. Can't help you in any way. Just not the type.'

Basti abruptly indicates the door. 'Your new abode has been arranged. I've been wiring to various parties but, as you know, Mr Smythe-Hippet, most oddly, did not get my missives. This will be rectified immediately. Please wait in the foyer. I sent down the note thinking it may . . . quell you. Obviously this was not the case, and then you all started . . . *swarming.* Everywhere.' He shudders in disgust, gathers himself. 'There will be food waiting at your new abode. To linger will only encourage you. You can wait by the cobra. In strict silence and stillness so as not to alarm her. Good day.'

It's like I've been winded. But a dragon's roaring, from deep inside, it bubbles up until I have to let it out –

'We thought we were getting a *family*. A new home. Some stability in our life. We loved being on the station by ourselves but that was because we knew there was always someone who . . . who . . . loved us.'

'We thought you'd adopt us!' Scruff butts in.

Basti holds up his hand, batting us away. 'You're to be sent to a very fine institution. Immediately. In all comfort. I'll even throw in some gifts from Harrods. My butler will arrange everything . . .'

Fiercely I grab Pin's trembling little hand. It's not gifts we want, not Harrods, it's a home. '*Please*, sir, we can't.'

'Oh yes you can. The only alternative is going to live with an acquaintance of mine, one Darius Davenport, who works in a funeral parlour near Brompton Cemetery and prepares cadavers for the grave.' Bert squeals in excitement and he looks at her, befuddled. '*That* is what you'll be doing if you do not go downstairs immediately and wait for transportation.' A curious lizard is firmly poked back into his pocket, as if this heated conversation is far too rough for its delicate constitution.

'*Nooooooooooooooooooooooooooooo!*' My full-throttle desert roar. I whip out Dad's war pistol in one hand; slingshot in the other.

It's the signal. Scruff pulls out his slingshot, Bert takes out Dad's hunting knife, Pin holds up both hands in the air like a gorilla and lets out his most piercing war cry. I aim the pistol right at Basti. He whips off his glasses, eyes wide. Starts breathing panicky, loud, fast; clutches his chest as if it hurts then stumbles out of the room, as quick as he can.

'Charlie Boo!' he yells wildly, desperately. 'Charlie Boo! Where are you? Come back. I need you! *I can't do this!*'

We are stunned. Can't move. Shocked into stillness like statues. Don't know what to do, where to go from here. We stare at each other, whispering our bewilderment, trying to work it out. What to do? Suddenly a door slams, from way below us. I wince. It sounds, sickeningly, like the huge front one.

We've been abandoned.

We stare at each other. Lower our weapons.

'He's gone,' whispers Bert in astonishment.

No. We look around. *Yes*.

So. Alone. All over again. Just like that. Maybe there really *is* a problem with us? All alone in an agitated, whispering, hissing house. And not very friendly hissing at this moment.

'Cuddle?' Pin asks fearfully.

I scoop him up because maybe there's a saltwater croc behind one of those wooden doors, or rats in the kitchen sink and snakes in the chandeliers. Our backs prickle up. If we head off through any door in this place we might be swallowed up, bitten, strangled or stung, never to return and never to find a way out – and four little skeletons might be found, years later, curled into balls in some obscure corner.

Scruff's whimpering now. We press tighter.

The portraits glare all around us, terrifyingly stern and admonishing, as if the four of us have badly let the family down. I suddenly realise that every single painting has a reptile in it somewhere – a snake on a brooch, a lizard on a shoe buckle – but none of that's helping us now because outside the door are several hundred creatures of very cold blood including, of course, one very large cobra. Right by the only known way out. With one very small clasp holding it in. A cobra that gives the appearance of licking its lips, in anticipation, whenever we're in sight.

Pin tries to climb onto my back as if it's the safest place in the world, and Bert joins him.

'Woo-oooo . . .' I wobble and tumble and we end up on the floor, giggling despite ourselves in one big jumbly heap.

'Come on, you lot, we've *got* to make this work,' I resolve.

I haul everyone up. Brush them down. Straighten their hair. Stand by the door, assess. The hissings grow louder, as if the mere presence of young flesh is infecting every single creature and whipping them into a frenzy. Deep breath. This has to be done.

I'm off! Whizzing across the room once again. 'Down, down!' I urge, guessing ground level's our best bet; no plan but no one needs to know that. We scramble down the ladders, slingshots in teeth, only to be stopped by the most terrifying sight . . .

The cobra's cage door, wide open.

Its occupant gone.

Snake on the loose. *Deadly* snake on the loose!

'Okay. Okay. Okay. We . . . ah . . .' I glance wildly around.

'Outside.' Scruff points to the front door. 'Kicky, quick. We've got to save him.'

'Who?'

'Basti!'

'Why?'

'Because he said he hasn't been out of the house for years. And everything's completely changed. Bombs have dropped, buildings are gone, the world's been turned upside down. He'll be petrified. Lost.'

I snort in disgust.

'He's family, Kick. The only bit of family we've got. We need to stick together.'

Bert suddenly pushes me from behind, willing me out after Scruff. I run my hand through my hair – right, great, someone else to look after now. Just add him to the list. And a frightful someone at that. Worse than Bert – who would have thought?

'*You* forced him outside,' Scruff adds. As brothers do.

'We all did, mate.'

'Basti, where are you?' Pin wails. 'I want you.' Obviously not getting a single thing about the past twenty minutes.

'If we lose him we lose the key to Dad.' Bert looks at me accusingly. 'It'll be your fault.'

'All right,' I sigh, 'all right.'

The four of us sprint as fast as we've ever sprinted in our lives, out into the shivery, slippery London street. No time for any waiting cobras to slither from a cupboard let alone grab us by the legs, no time to wonder who Charlie Boo is, no time to ponder whether we're dressed correctly for a bitter London night, no time to wonder if we're mad, deluded, about to fall into a trap . . . Basti might be leading us straight through the gates of an orphanage for all we know.

But he's family. They're right.

'Come on,' Bert yells. 'Chaaaaaaaaaaaaaarge!'

Dad's hunting knife – rust or blood still on it because I refuse to take whatever it is off – leads the way.

7
CALAMITY AND
COMMOTION

Not a soul in sight.

Suddenly, a great screech of traffic noise. Brakes squealing, horns blaring. Yelling, screaming. We look towards the bottom of the hill. A huge commotion's going on at an intersection there; a great mad cacophony of life.

'Basti,' Scruff whispers.

'Bas-teeee!' Pin squeals. And he's off as fast as his fat little legs will carry him.

The rest of us wince, know with sickening certainty what's next – he's off on another grand Pin-adventure, his Pin-curiosity unleashed. But the hill's steep, it's getting dark. Plop! Yep, he's down. Flat on his front with a horrible thud. He picks himself up without so much as a whimper and continues his fearless charge, just as he does at home.

'I'm coming, Basteeeeeeee!'

What can we do? Nothing but follow. We thunder down the steep slope of Campden Hill Square.

And there, in the middle of a traffic intersection at the bottom, is our uncle. Standing among a huge crammed crowd of terrified and indignant pedestrians and drivers and passengers, who are all shaking their fists and screaming, their cars and buses and bikes and trucks halted, stuck. And these people aren't shouting and shrilling because a man in a red velvet coat is standing, dazed, in the middle of winter, in the middle of their very busy avenue . . . oh no. They're shouting and shrilling because this man has a very large cobra wrapped around his body. A cobra that's puffing its neck, and flicking its tongue, and lashing out in a most terrifying way. As if it's about to strike anyone who gets too close.

Sssssss!

'Bas-ti!' Pin claps his hands in delight.

Bert makes a beeline for the snake, thrilled, ready for her big starring moment: the Great Uncle Rescue. Ready for the adulation of the crowd. I yank her back.

The situation's not good.

The crowd's closing in. They want their dinners and warmth and they're late. They've just been through six long years of war, they're jittery and suspicious and tired and they don't want any scary new surprises in their lives; they just want a quiet, unthreatening Christmas this time around, it's all they can bear.

The cobra's getting increasingly furious; the crowd louder, jumpier; Basti's in the midst of it just staring, bewildered and oblivious, at the war damage around him – as if he had absolutely no idea. He looked so terrifying and imperious in his own house but now, outside, he looks shrunken. Befuddled. Almost like a child.

Lost. Completely, utterly lost. Just like us.

I step towards him. Can't help it. He needs someone. The grown-ups are getting angrier, there's roaring and bellowing, children are screaming, babies wailing. A stone's thrown. Ow! Another. It strikes Basti's leg and he snaps out of his gaze, looks around wildly.

I can read him, he doesn't know what to do; his hands fluster to the snake, he needs calm for his unpredictable pet and he's not getting it anywhere. He needs to retreat, find quiet, but it's like he's frozen. Dogs strain their leashes, desperate to take on the creature that's lashing out with fury at anyone who gets too close, hissing and flashing its fangs.

No one knows how to proceed. This cluster of Londoners has endured all manner of horrors over the past six years – Horatio's told us about homes smashed to smithereens and fire storms of intense heat and whistling doodlebugs dropping from the sky and buses falling into craters and men not coming home and sudden orphans and endless sleepless nights – but these people never had to deal with this before: a live cobra in the middle of their street.

The angry crowd inches closer, screaming for some kind of resolution to this most bizarre of traffic jams. An invasion of an utterly different sort but an invasion nonetheless. And they're not having a bar of it. Who knows where a snake will end up.

There's a deafening whine. We cover our ears; the noise hurts in our heads.

'Siren!' Scruff yells, and he dives for the ground.

Horns blast, people shout, a police van screeches to a halt.

'Get up,' hisses Bert, 'the war's *over*.'

Ten officers pour out ready for a fight. Catch sight of what they're dealing with and, as one, reel back.

Collect themselves.

Everything goes deathly quiet; everyone holds their breath.

The men circle Basti in his slippers and flying cap; batons raised, swaying with menace. 'Stay back!' the tallest policeman suddenly barks. 'Everyone – back!'

We most certainly obey. Oh yes. Because no one wants to get *too* close to a cobra; no one wants it biting them or swallowing them or whatever those creatures do; no one wants it slithering off into the wilds of Holland Park to suddenly reappear in a school satchel or a lavatory or (gasp) a bed.

Three policemen clamber from the van and creep forward with some kind of long, huge weapony thing over their shoulders. My mouth goes dry. This means business and not the good kind. It's aimed straight at Basti.

'A bazooka,' Scruff whispers in awe. 'No, couldn't be. But something like it. Maybe? I don't know. Dad told me about them, Kick. He saw them in North Africa in May 1943. But surely not, here.'

'I've got no idea,' I rasp. 'But whatever it is, I do not like it.'

'Maybe it's got sleeping gas in it. Or a net. Or poison darts. Or something . . .'

Scruff lowers his slingshot, can't compete. Because this terrifyingly huge and effective-looking weapon – whatever it is – looks like it's been captured from the Eastern Front and that the men behind it are just itching to try it out. Basti looks even more odd and bewildered now, in front of the officers; completely out of place but with a deadly weapon wrapped about his neck.

'No,' I whisper, hand over mouth in horror. 'Don't do anything silly. Please, Basti, please.'

Because Scruff's right, he's our closest living relative, the only person we've got in this country – and this terrible situation he's found himself in is all our fault.

'Bang bang!' Pin jumps up and down with excitement, not helping matters in the slightest.

Basti suddenly catches sight of the weapon. Stands like a rabbit frozen in headlights, trembling, staring as if transfixed, his face deathly white like he's seen a ghost.

'I –' He stumbles, addressing it. 'I was just looking for, for Charlie Boo . . .'

He starts shaking. No longer able to speak. Stuck again. And it's obvious none of the adults have a clue what to do next: if Basti falls, his cobra will be on the loose . . . and *no one* wants that.

It's a stand-off. Policemen: paralysed. Basti: paralysed. And me?

Sharply propelled forward by two sets of Bert knuckles firmly on my bottom. 'It's our chance, Kick. Come on.'

'Kicky, fix!' Pin commands.

'It's this or the orphanage,' Scruff adds.

I look at them in panic. Right. So. No choice then, eh? Lick my lips. Step forward. 'Uncle? We're here. We're taking you home.'

Deathly silence. Walking on eggshells. You could hear a pin drop. It's as if everyone senses that something very peculiar is going on here. Slowly, slowly Basti turns. Raises one eyebrow.

At least he's listening.

'Come on,' I coax. '*Everyone's* waiting for you. They miss you. They need you.'

'Home,' Scruff echoes wistfully.

Basti's other eyebrow raises.

'We're here now,' I say firmly. 'We've arrived. To help you.'

Once again I reach out my hand to him. Once again it's unshaken, just hovering in thin air. The sting of that, all over again. I bite my lip but it will not stop me. I step closer to Basti, to the snake.

'Careful,' someone in the crowd pleads in horror, 'that thing could kill you.'

Basti stares at the four of us then the ring of

policemen then the crowd then us once more – trying to work out which is the best bet. All equally traumatic. The tension's as tight as a stretched rubber band.

My hand's still stuck out. I will not lower it. The cobra hisses in fury as if it's going to bite something, anything, any second, can hardly contain itself; the crowd gasps in horror, steps back. In a trance I move forward, barely thinking, barely knowing what I'm doing. I step right up close and stroke the snake on the back of its neck: 'There you go, girl, there there.' Dad's taught me how to handle them, on our private hunting expeditions, just him and me – 'because you have to protect the family, Kicketty, when I'm not there, I'm relying on you' – and it's all coming back.

Basti's rigid. Just his eyes swivel to me and the cobra, in amazement.

The bazooka men inch closer. The tallest policeman raises his hand, signalling me to vacate, fast. He's losing patience, something needs to happen here quick.

I whisper to Basti, 'Come home,' and slip back, hoping he'll follow.

He doesn't move.

The policeman shrills a whistle around his neck. Basti's transfixed, can't run, can't remove the snake, is stuck. No, Basti, *no*!

The policeman gives the signal to fire –

'I love my uncle! Hip hip hooray for the snake man of Holland Park!'

It's Bert, clapping her hands madly and jumping up and down. Everyone turns, distracted, at this crazy intervention. The bazooka men lower their bazooka thing and team Caddy seizes its chance: Pin runs to his uncle with little arms outstretched and grabs him around the legs; Scruff dashes forward and gives him the most radiant smile (the one his father says that no one but his family can ever resist) and I grab the opening: step forward calmly, strongly, a hand once again outstretched.

'I'm taking you home.' Firm. Reassuring. I smile – crooked as usual, one side up one side down, just like Dad's, everyone tells me that; that with my hair chopped off I could be him.

Basti looks at me intently, head cocked. Relaxes. Uncurls his cobra. Hugs it like it's now the cheekiest of kittens. Smiles and nods apologetically at the crowd – 'Good evening to you all, terribly sorry' – and walks mildly towards his brand new nieces and nephews.

Just like that.

We've got him.

A family, at last.

And yes, I am now trying to pretend that a man with a deadly snake beside me is the most normal thing in the world – la la la, happens all the time. Jolly good, yes yes. Everyone lets out a sigh of relief.

'He's with us,' I declare loudly to all and sundry. 'We're taking him home.'

'He's our uncle,' Scruff adds, with something like pride.

I explain to the policeman in charge that this most esteemed man is, actually, a world expert on exotic snakes. Of the subcontinent. A most renowned member, in fact, of the Royal Geographical Society. (Dad was always ending his wonderfully wild bedtime stories about wrestling piranhas in the Amazon and outswimming white pointers off Cape Horn with a lecture on his latest escapade at that hallowed institution; he was always getting me to read accounts of Livingstone and Stanley and Shackleton and Scott and the place was always mentioned by those men; Dad dreamed all his life of being a most honoured member of the Society – 'The roguish Aussie one, in his old bush hat, the most adventurous adventurer of the lot!')

And yes indeed, Mr Police Officer, of course there's a permit to keep this totally harmless specimen in our uncle's house. 'Which he never leaves. Ever. But there's been, um, a slight mistake. And this situation will never happen again. It's now firmly under control. Thank you very much. Good evening to you.'

'Right, Miss. Yes. What – hang on – what are you saying?' The policeman's spinning, trying to keep a handle on everything – answer me, the spectators, his men, and get the traffic moving, the good citizens of Kensington home – but I'm off in the confusion, grabbing Basti's elbow and steering him away, quick smart, before the crowd puts two and two together. Before they demand the, er, elimination of the deadly creature in their midst and the immediate search of the house it comes from and then – horror – finding out what else is in there and – gulp – demanding a swift disbandment of the entire operation.

Imagine. The Kensington Reptilarium shut down. Just like that. After years and years of operation. Just as Basti predicted: that we will *fatally* draw attention to it.

'Quick,' I whisper to Scruff, 'we need to disappear. Fast. Grab Pinny.'

The crowd murmurs; cars and trucks begin to move off; three men in pinstripe suits argue that there really should be arrests here, this gentleman should be taken into custody and his house – wherever it is, it must be close – be declared a danger zone. 'Gentlemen, you must act.' Their voices are rising most alarmingly as we slip away to a cluster of enormous, black looming trees, what looks like a wild and impenetrable park.

We flit past huge trunks, breathing fast, until we find ourselves in a clearing among the ruins of a beautiful old house: smashed to pieces, abandoned, its pale stone ghostly in the dark.

'Oh,' Basti keeps saying with infinite sadness. 'Oh.' As if he can hardly bear the sight.

'How do we get out of here?' I ask. 'We need to get home. Safe. All of us.'

'This way,' Basti says, and swiftly he leads us through a small building whose smashed skeleton is some columns of bricks and whose flesh is the air, the sky. 'But this was the orangerie!' he cries. 'No. And these, the stables, twenty-four horses, they had, and two donkeys, just for us. And this, a most charming folly –'

His hand is at his mouth; he is spinning around in wonder and shock. It's been years since he left his house, of course, and the world beyond it has been utterly transformed. Forever. Obliterated, and there's no going back. It's all in his face.

'Basti, we need to move fast,' I urge gently. 'The police might be following.'

He leads us on through a maze of trees in the thick, spooky dark; surefooted, certain, swift, like he's done this a thousand times before. As a child, I bet. Now we're out in a steep, cobbled lane; we cut through an alley between two houses and voila, we're in Campden Hill Square again with the Reptilarium rising in dilapidated splendour at its crest. I lead the way up the steep hill, quick, before anyone can take note of exactly where we're going.

'Snakey! Here, snakey!' Bert squeals in joy at the cobra and mimes wrapping it around her neck, her new winter accessory. How to keep her away from it . . . how to stay with Basti . . . how to get warm, and fed. So much to think about, so many people to worry over and we're not even inside yet, hurry everyone, *hurry*!

The snake flicks its tongue, right at Bert. She shivers with glee. Pin walks backwards in front of the lot of us, arms wide, beaming. At his brand new uncle, at his sister's snakey delight, at his brother's bare feet in the freezing cold, at his funny fierce biggest sister who's always making everything right. As she does.

I smile back. Because this crazy posse around me is the start of a brand new family. A brand new life. Jumbly and ragtag and reluctant and impossible and scruffy and contradictory as it is, it's *family*, yes. Pin's puffed up by the very idea, full of chuff, and I can just tell he's going to make the most of it.

We all are. Because we must. However peculiar this new family might be.

As long as Basti agrees we can now stay . . . this is the main thing to think about of all the things roaring in my head this night. He *has* to. He'd better not change his mind once the door is shut. I'd better not let him through it first. I stare at his back. Do I trust . . . no, can't. Quite. Just can't. We've saved him, but who knows if that counts for anything in this new life . . .

8

THE REPTILARIUM, NO THE SQUARE, NO CLARIDGES, NO THE...

'**So we can stay?**'

I'm enquiring cheekily as we trudge up the hill.

'Er . . .' Basti stumbles.

'Just for the night?' Scruff jumps in.

'But this wasn't in the plan.'

'Just for a little while?' Bert pleads.

'The orphanage awaits. Didn't I say that already? A rather luxurious one, I might add. Much better than what I could ever provide.'

'We're starving,' I announce firmly.

'There's absolute nothing to feed the desert variety of child, I'm afraid. No goanna guts, no witchetty grubs.'

'We'd settle for some porridge!' Scruff exclaims.

Basti does not take the bait.

'Freeeeeeeeeeeeezing. Any chance of some new clothes?' Bert, of course.

Basti shakes his head. 'Nothing that fits.'

'Naming no names, troops –' I look at them all '– but some of us might be in need of a snuggly bed and a kiss goodnight. It's been a long day.'

'I do not provide kisses nor snuggles nor touching of any variety, nor warmth, for that matter. You would be sorely disappointed hanging about with the likes of me.'

Good grief. It's like the closer we get to the Reptilarium, the more obvious it is the building's got some strange kind of power over Basti, pulling him in, changing him; he's turning more and more into his old, cantankerous self. Nup. Not on. He *owes* us for the past twenty minutes.

I stand in front of him. Hands on hips. 'We just saved you, mate.'

He looks at me in horror: desert variety of girl-child = absolutely terrifying.

'For which I am eternally grateful, young . . . er . . . lady? It is a lady, isn't it?' He lifts his glasses and peers; raises an eyebrow, examining close. 'Actually, you could be rather fetching if one could somehow extract you from under all those layers of dirt. Rather

fetching indeed. You just need to be chiselled out.'
With the end of his glasses he gingerly lifts a matted
piece of my hair – it's quite a stick. 'Hmm. Rather
too close for comfort to a bird's nest. Good for the
rats, I suppose.'

I turn brusquely away, scowling, hurting; not
changing for anyone, not even Dad and didn't he
try. I liked looking like him. He didn't get it. 'Your
mum was such a lady,' he'd sigh. Well, I'm not.
Don't want a bar of it; lace and frills and perfume
and hairbrushes and sighing and giggling and boys
and whatnot, no time for any of it.

'Actually, I'm not sure if there's a young lady in
there at all,' Basti sighs, dropping the matted hair
in defeat.

'I don't want to be "chiselled out", thank you very
much. I'm happy the way I am and far too busy to be
something as silly as a girl. Too busy rescuing uncles.
Hmm, yes, that's right. And finding shelter for my
little brothers and sister and keeping our family
together and –'

'You don't have to, Kick,' Bert jumps in, 'really.'

I push her. She stamps on my foot.

'Temper temper,' Basti admonishes me. 'I've heard
all about it, Miss Kick. And I do not relish it. Or any
type of physical fight, from any of you. Or noise, or

squealing, or shouting, or talk. So this, I'm afraid, is where I depart – quick smart.' He walks backwards, fast, hands out in horror at the lot of us.

I stamp my foot. He's as contradictory and changeable as . . . as . . . me. And I will win this.

'Look out!' Scruff yells.

Too late.

'Ow! I *say*.'

Basti's just bumped smack bang into that terribly glamorous neighbour who's now head to toe in tiger print – hat, boots and coat – and staggering down the hill with an enormous box she can barely see over the top of. She stops as if she's seen a ghost. As if she absolutely cannot *believe* what's in front of her.

'Sebastian? Is it . . . *you*? Outside?' She's shaking her head in wonder. 'Well, I never.'

Basti snaps up his glasses. Eyes widen in surprise. Snaps them down again. The neighbour blushes. Steps back. Drops her box in a flurry of confusion and hundreds of little white candles fall out and tumble roly-poly down the hill, gleefully running away from the lot of us. Fast.

'Uuuuuuuurghhhh,' she yells in frustration and she's off running furiously, swooping on as many candles as she can in her tall tiger heels.

'Troops – run!' I grab little white sticks left, right and centre.

Everyone joins in except for Basti, who just stands there, bewildered, with a snake wrapped around his neck; he starts pointing to any candle still on the loose, directing. 'There . . . over here, boy . . . under the Roller, quick!'

Scruff's so keen he slides into a tummy-dive; Pin's managed just two candles, which he's now trying to stick in his ears; Bert's got a sarong full. When the candles are back in their box the neighbour says thank you, to the four of us, then just stares pointedly at the culprit.

I know that look. I've seen it on Mum, years ago. At Dad. I'd forgotten it until now. One of those glares that has years and years of things said and not said and it's all too hard and someone's right cranky at someone but no one's saying anything; no one's diving in and clearing it up. Grown-ups, they're *so* complicated. Who'd want to be one.

'Well, well,' the woman says. Finally.

A very long pause. As if these two people have a huge amount to say to each other but never will. Basti just stands there, nervously stroking his snake. He's breathing jaggedly but trying not to. He's agitated, lost for talk.

'Basti?' I prompt.

He glares at me in annoyance: back off.

Bert goes up to him and clutches his hand then turns her eyes coolly on his neighbour, warning her away, girl to girl.

The neighbour waves a single candle at them both. 'You've forgotten what these are for, haven't you, Sebastian?' Her tongue clucks in annoyance. 'Or can't be bothered.' She glances around the square. '*Your* house – please don't make it the only dark one this year. The only one, year after year. This is our ritual, remember, and you haven't done it since 1919. Oh yes, I've been taking note. And every year I've prayed for . . . a miracle. That you'd somehow change. Be what you were. Spring back into life. Somehow.' She sighs, in hopelessness, looking at him with the most peculiar expression. 'And the rest of us of course haven't lit the candles for six endless years, blackouts and all that. But we need to now. Urgently. More than ever –' She stops, clogged. 'After Europe, after everything that's gone on.' Her voice drops to a whisper. 'The camps. Have you seen the pictures? We *need* the lights in the windows, Sebastian, this year of all years. Please.' A pause. 'Are you even listening?'

No one speaks.

'It's the not *knowing*, Seb. The never knowing . . . with us.'

She's almost crying, the air is prickly with it.

'Sebastian?'

Silence. She flings the candle back in the box.

Our uncle just stands there, stroking his snake, looking at his pet and no one else, in a world of his own. The reptile hisses and lashes out.

The lady groans in fury and storms off. '*Why* did I think it'd be any different this time around? Why?'

'Will you adopt us,' Scruff yells out after her, 'if our uncle doesn't work out? Like – maybe – tonight? Really quick?'

The woman freezes at the word 'adopt', her back still to us. 'And what are you doing with . . . *children* . . . of all things?' Her voice is icy. 'You? I can imagine it when you were younger but . . . now?'

Basti looks wounded. 'My nephews and nieces,' he cries after her. 'They've been sent to me because . . . because . . .' He turns in panic to the lovely home we're standing outside, notices a Christmas tree in its window, a holly wreath on its door, peers, as if he hasn't seen any of this for years. 'Because of Christmas, if you must. They're family. And they're here . . . with me, yes me . . . for it.'

Well well, what a scene: four Caddys leaping into the air, yelling and whooping with the joyiest joy you've ever seen in your life. Because we're *staying*! Christmas is coming! Everything will be all right!

'What?' It's spat. As if to her this is the most ridiculous arrangement in the world.

We stop.

'In *your* home? Do you even know when Christmas is? What you do?'

'Er, well –'

'And what will you be feeding them, pray? Roasted rattlesnake? Mouse-tail spaghetti? Would you like that, children, would you? Most delicious, hmm?'

'I –' Basti splutters.

'And presents? A snakeskin, perhaps? A desiccated rat?' The woman is now back with us, bending down, whispering, 'I'm so frightfully sorry,' as if whatever's ahead is rather terrible for children and she knows it. She cups her hand under Bert's chin, strokes it in pity, then hands to each of us a single white candle. 'Merry Christmas, my dears. He was fun, once. But those days have long gone. Good luck.' And then she walks off. As fast she can. 'And for Pete's sakes, Sebastian, get them *dressed*,' she yells like a headmistress, without looking back. 'There must be something in that attic.'

Two elderly neighbours walk past.

'Helen, Rupert,' she calls to them, 'look, it's Basti, he's out and about, can you believe it?' She's choked up with emotion. 'And he's having family over for Christmas, how extraordinary.'

'Oh Basti, dear Basti, you're finally stepping out!' says the elderly woman, with gladness. 'We're so frightfully happy you've . . . recovered. Your mother would be so pleased, dear boy. Such a kindly soul, as are you. *Were* you. She'd be so happy to have her darling boy back.' A pause. 'Yes?'

Basti shakes his head, backs away, from all of them, all of us. The neighbours shake their heads sadly, bewildered, as if they know they're pushing their luck with this. Basti turns from them without a word, and they disappear swiftly into the dark, embarrassed, awkward.

Leaving the five of us alone once again.

'*NOOOoooooooooooo!*' I cry.

All the normality in our lives. Vanished in the dark.

Pin's bottom lip trembles, he's about to launch into a huge wail. I know what he's thinking: it'll be fried rat in a few days, a snakeskin wrapped in newspaper, gecko porridge, iguana cake – Christmas is absolutely hopeless, as is just about everything in this new life.

'Mouse-tail sketti?' he sobs, looking up at his uncle. 'Uncle Basti?'

The man can't answer. He just looks at us Caddy kids, absolutely stuck. Runs both hands through his hair in frustration. How did he get himself into this? 'I can't ... I don't ...' he stumbles. 'I didn't mean to –'

'What?' I snap. 'What? Invite us over for Christmas, perhaps? Was that a most horrible mistake? That you're about to withdraw?'

Basti can't answer, he looks at us helplessly.

Pin's now howling like a child lost in a crowd at a country fair.

'She's right,' whispers Scruff, 'he can't do it.'

And now we're all imagining the Christmas ahead: an uncle who doesn't want us one bit, no proper presents, no laughter, no cuddles and most of all, no Dad. No tossing in the air, one by one. No sleeping in his bed, the five of us at once. No Peter Pan airplanes as he holds us as flat as ironing boards and zooms us around in bright air. No magic coins appearing from behind ears, no gum from the Yanks. No bedtime stories of Santas arriving on camels and wombats and crocs, and no camping expeditions to sacred sites – 'Don't walk on them, tiger cubs, we must respect that' – and no piggybacks because the sand is too hot for any of us but Dad's feet are as tough 'as old Bible leather, chaps!' No slingshots carefully whittled, four of them, in descending size, with names carefully engraved in cursive script and lined up as obedient as soldiers on the mantelpiece.

Nope, absolutely none of it.

Just four tiny white candles. Our only gifts in a new Christmas of vast bleakness. With an uncle who's trying his best to be rid of us. Who doesn't have a clue. About *anything*. Who loves snakes more than people and it seems has never touched anyone in his life.

Pin's happy little soldier's heart is quite, quite cracked. Scruff's not far behind.

'What are you going to do, Kick?' Bert asks.

I look her straight in the eyes. 'This, sis. This.'

I pick up a stick and hurl it into the garden square like I'm flinging a desert spear to shatter a mirage, to wake us all up. I've had enough. I need this new life to go away and the old one back, the one where I don't have to be the grown-up any more. We have to find Horatio and demand our old world back. Get to the bottom of the mystery of Dad; storm War Offices, whatever, if we must.

I grab Pin in one hand, Bert in the other. She seizes Scruff on the way. The lot of us march smartly down the hill, smartly into our brand new life. Where? What? Goodness knows. *Anything* but this. We'll find Horatio somewhere, even if it means camping on his doorstep; he'll sort this out.

'Where are you taking us?' Bert cries.

'Home.'

'But . . . where's that?' Scruff says in dismay. 'I'm starving, I'll die if we don't eat, we've only just . . .'

'I *know* what I'm doing! Troops, onward march!'

I yank them hard. When I'm angry nothing can stop me.

Except, er, several policemen.

At the bottom of the square. Crossing the street. With intent.

Right.

Policemen, no less, who were at the standoff. Who look like they're now trying to find the house with the cobra in it. Like they've visited a lot of other streets. They're waving their torches, peering through the garden square as if this could possibly be the logical place for a man with a snake.

They mustn't see us. Under any circumstances. The Reptilarium might shut down if they get us, someone will crack if we're caught. I gasp with sudden realisation: it's the only thing we've now got in our lives and Basti will be left with nothing but the shell of a life. Our escape is blocked, there's only one place to go.

'Troops, about-turn!' I whisper in panic. Quick smart I turn everyone around and quick smart march them straight back up the hill.

A lone figure, dead ahead of us.

Uncle Basti.

Slowly walking to his Reptilarium. Looking so terribly all-by-himself, so much smaller and bowed and older and . . . sad . . . yes, that. He walks past his neighbour's house without so much as a glance, just continues on to his home.

Bert peels away, then Scruff; they both run straight up to him. Pin follows and I'm not far behind. We swarm around our uncle – 'We're here!' 'We're back!' – and you know what, the smile of relief on him, in the gloom, is like sunlight suddenly bursting through a storm cloud. He wipes an eye. Has he been . . . *crying*? Surely not. No.

Yes?

'I'm sorry,' he whispers hoarsely. 'I'm all of a . . . mess.'

Grown-ups. You just can't work them out.

9
THE LEGEND OF CAMPDEN HILL SQUARE

'Last one to the door's a rotten egg!'

Scruff's shouting and we're all dashing for it as fast as we can. Beaten, most astonishingly, by Basti, who's like a horse straining under the reins at the sight of home. He whoops in triumph, flings open the door and slams it resoundingly shut on the world. With us – hallelujah! – on the right side of it.

'*One* night, Miss Kick,' he warns me.

'Yaaaaaay!'

The reptiles in the building bristle with affronted hisses and rustles, as if they're jealous, as I try to shush my lot down.

'One *only*. And you will all have to prove that you're the right type of species to spend a night in this hallowed place. No one else, apart from Charlie Boo, has ever passed the Reptilarium test.'

'Who's Charlie Boo?' Bert asks.

'Only *the* most talented butler in the entire British Empire. Trained in Rangoon. The best of the best.'

'The Reptilarium test? I love tests! My dad says my whole presence is a test,' Scruff declares proudly.

'I'm sure he does,' Basti purrs. 'Just you wait, Master Scruff; I have something especially for you.' He narrows his eyes and smiles inscrutably at him.

I grab Pin's hand. Our uncle's so changeable, unknowable, unguessable. Can we trust what's ahead? Who's the real him?

'Now, if you pass, there may well be a bed of some sort for the evening. And a meal of similar – rustic – improvisation.' He bends down to Pin. 'And I promise you it will *not* be mouse-tail spaghetti, Master Phineas.'

Pin shivers all over in delight.

'And there may well be a visit to the attic to conjure up some appropriate items of clothing. There must be something up there. Haven't visited for years. Azure blue, young lady.' He points to my ragged top.

'Pardon?'

'Your colour. The colour of that wretched sky over your way. And I do believe there's some cocoa in the house for any chocolate lovers who could, possibly, be in our midst.'

Scruff punches the air. *'Yes.'*

Bert clears her throat.

'Miss Albertina!' Basti hits his head in frustration. 'How could one possibly forget? Black black black. Well, there's most certainly that upstairs. In abundance. And I may even have a spare coffin up there for the likes of you to sleep in. You'd like that, wouldn't you?'

She claps her hands in glee; I step back, not liking this coffin talk.

'Now, who's afraid of heights?'

I step back further.

With a flourish Basti indicates an enormous lever by the door – we didn't notice it before. Pulls it with great effort. 'Your first test,' he purrs.

Four kids, open-mouthed, gazing up at a giant steel arm emerging from the top door of the tower with a great whirring sound. A wooden seat is swinging from it, suspended by four chains. Basti directs it as the chair zooms down through the vast space and stops right by us. It jiggles expectantly. Jiggles again.

'Who's first?' Basti enquires.

'What is it?' I ask softly, my hand firm on Scruff, who's champing at the bit.

'Oh, just some little thing I dreamt up, for when I get too creaky to climb the ladders. I've spent *years* perfecting this Reptilarium, young lady. Nothing must stop the smooth functioning of this establishment. Especially four little rock wallabies from the bush.'

We cram into the seat together, Pin on my lap, Bert on Scruff's.

'It wasn't meant for four,' Basti murmurs, 'but oh well, we'll soon find out,' and he secures a chain across us, whispers 'hold tight' then dashes back to the lever. With an almighty groan the chains lift the chair into the air, as if they can barely support this new weight. Then ... whoooooooooooosh! The seat shoots up to the ceiling.

'Wheeeeeeeeeee!' Pin squeals.

Bert and I hold onto anything and everything, for dear life, then all four of us stare down from our vantage point under the dome, swinging gently.

'I feel kind of sick,' Bert says.

'Not now!' Scruff.

'Don't look down!' Me.

The chains suddenly drop a few metres; they're straining to hold our weight. We scream.

Basti's unconcerned. 'Now, who would you like to visit first?' he shouts up at us. 'My taipan,

Frederica? You'll be holding her by the end of the night, Master Scruff. The twin rattlesnakes, Osbert and Oswald? Dicken, my grumpy komodo dragon? The Reptilarium is all yours . . . for one night and one night only. Children, it's what you wanted. May the test commence!'

'Is there a Loch Ness monster somewhere in here? Can I stroke him too?' Yes, that would be Scruff.

'Not quite, but allow me, if you please.'

And with a lurch we're off, whizzing in huge circles, spiralling to all the different levels, stopping in at various cages.

'You can do it yourself, Miss Kick. There's a control lever to your left,' Basti instructs.

I lean over, find a small brass knob. We jerk wildly in the air; Pin screams; Bert demands a go.

'It's extremely sensitive!' Basti shouts. 'Just a gentle tap.'

After several wildly jerky stop-starts we're off, zinging round and round the enormous space with the wind in our hair.

Wheeeeeeeeeeee!

Pin starts laughing wildly, it's the most beautiful sound, then Scruff, Bert and finally myself; we can't stop. Because we're suddenly kids again, proper kids, letting go and not worrying and just having proper, silly fun, just like at home, for the first time since our world was turned upside down. Bert's squeezing me in exhilaration, saying 'Come on, Kicky girl!'; Scruff's urging, 'Fast, faster,' and suddenly my eyes are prickling up – because I'm happy – for the first time in so long.

Cracked. By kindness.

We *so* needed it.

The swing glides slowly past a candle. Scruff reaches for it, snatches it up – and drops it.

Nooooooooooooooooooooo!

Right onto the cobra's cage. Still, miraculously, lit.

Basti yelps; the snake reels, hissing and rearing in terror; wax drips dangerously close.

'*This* is why I never want children in my life!' Basti thunders, red with rage, instantly changed. He whips off his jacket and throws it on the cage. The flame's snuffed. The snake thuds crazily against the bars as if it's been struck by burning wax. Basti extracts it, flings up the chair lever and then storms off, slamming a door somewhere on the ground level.

Leaving us dangling. Alone. In silence.

Er, right. The control on my chair won't work now. Of course. Panicky, I jiggle it. Again, and again. Nothing.

We're stuck. Fifty feet up.

'Sorry, Uncle Basti,' I cry to an empty house; Scruff follows suit.

No one emerges. No one responds. Just a lot of reptiles and it feels like they're laughing at us now; laughing and licking their lips; they've won.

'Baaaaaastiiiiiiiii?'

How long how are we meant to be up here? Is endurance part of the test? Are we staying up here all night?

'Nice one, troops,' Bert snaps sarcastically.

'I was looking forward to that hot chocolate.' Scruff sighs.

'And coffin.' Bert.

'I think we've failed the test,' Scruff rubs it in.

Pin starts to cry in mortification, and I soothe him, all the while peering down in panic and willing our uncle to appear. Nope. Right. Well and truly stuck here. For what feels like an eternity.

Pin's crying turns to sniffles then silence then suddenly he wraps his pudgy little arms around my neck – 'I love you, Kicky' – and I've never loved him back so fiercely in my life. But what to do? We dangle, wait, periodically yell, 'Basti.' Five minutes, ten, fifteen . . .

Pin starts to cry again.

Bert swings the swing wildly, viciously.

'Stop it!' I snap.

'What else is there to do?'

'We can . . . we can . . . *sing*! All of us. Come on.'

I launch into one of Dad's favourite songs, 'Bound for Botany Bay,' heartily, desperately, over and over; he used to get us singing it whenever we were afraid of something, loudly, crazily, to giggle us up and make us forget. The others join in, louder and louder until 'Too-ral-li-ooral-li-addity!' is ringing out under the glittery dome and then slowly, miraculously – 'Too-ral-li-ooral-li-ay!' – a head emerges from the slammed door; and slowly, miraculously, an uncle steps out. Walks to the lever by the front door, and gently drops us to the ground.

Pheeeeeeeeeeeeeeeeeeeew. We tumble out.

'I'm sorry.' Basti shakes his head, laughing helplessly, soft again. 'I'm not very good at . . . people. You see, it's been so long. I'm all rusty with it. Pushing you away and inviting you in and then storming off and doing it all over again. Oh dear . . . it's quite a mess, isn't it? All mixed up. So terribly hard for me, and you. I'm . . . sorry.'

I smile reassuringly. 'It's all right. Really. No one's perfect.'

Because Dad's always saying that, about himself, when another letter arrives from the bank; or from

Aunty Ethel, instructing him to just grow up and sort his children's lives out.

Basti smiles back in gratitude. 'Your father taught you that song, didn't he? He was a good man.'

'Yes,' I say, 'yes,' and without knowing why, just burst into tears.

Basti doesn't know how to react. His hand hovers near my face as if he wants to wipe away a tear but can't, quite, bring himself to do it.

'I . . . we . . .'

'Come on, troops,' Scruff says, firmly, 'let's get some cocoa. Don't we need it. *All* of us. Kicky?'

And with infinite gentleness he puts his arm around me. It's Basti's cue. He leads the way through a door to the kitchen. I've never loved my brother more, often feel like thumping him but right now just want to kiss him hugely in relief (he'd prefer the decking: less girl germs).

And that's how the four of us suddenly find ourselves sitting around an enormous kitchen table with an affronted-looking cobra before us in a huge cage.

'It's the Reptilarium Hospital in here,' Basti explains.

Scruff looks startled and guilty.

'She's all right, she just got a fright. Her name's Perdita, by the way.'

'Nice to meet you, Perdy.' Bert winks.

I'm desperate to steer the conversation away from annoying new house guests, wounded pets and failed tests. I ask Basti about the neighbour outside and her big cardboard box, and what were the candles all about?

He flinches, drops the spoon in the hot chocolate he's stirring. 'Blast!'

I leap up and help him fish it out; perhaps I should have stuck with wounded pets.

'There's a tradition, Kick,' he says abruptly. 'From 1898. There was a refuge here once.'

'What's a refuge?' Bert asks.

'When you say *no*!' Pin exclaims. Everyone laughs, even Basti, despite himself.

'No, not *refuse*, young man, although I do rather like that. It's a place that provides shelter. And there was a refuge, in this very square. For Jewish people. The owners put lit candles in the windows of their building, every Christmas Eve, as a secret signal. It meant that every lonely Jewish person without their family around them would always find a meal and a bed there, around that time; a home among strangers, so to speak. They just had to look out for the candles.'

'How marvellous!' I exclaim, a touch too longingly.

'Yes, quite.' Basti looks at me sharply. 'But then one night some people stoned the house. Smashed all the windows, every single one. It was terrifying and horrible.'

'How *awful*!'

'Yes. And the next Christmas Eve, each person living in this square decided to put candles in every one of their own windows. In solidarity. And the one after that, and the one after that. Every single house in this square, every single window. To say to the world that they wanted to hide the Jewish refuge among all their own places; so that any horrid outsiders who were thinking of stoning it wouldn't be able to work out exactly in *which* building the shelter was located. Ingenious, eh? But they'd tell any refugees that needed it where the magic building was.'

We're silent, spellbound.

'It worked. The refuge was never attacked again. And the tradition lives on to this day – well, apart from the past six years of blackouts – even though the shelter is long gone.'

'Amazing,' Bert whispers.

'Candles! Candles!' Scruff punches the air in excitement.

Pin runs madly around the table in anticipation, fuelled by cocoa, watched by Perdita. Can a reptile get dizzy? 'Where are they?' Pin declares, ready to troop off to each window in the house.

'But not every house, right?' I ask Basti softly, placing my hand over his. It's brushed off.

'No. Quite.'

And I just know, from that suddenly clipped voice, that we'll never get our uncle to light a candle on Christmas Eve, and most likely he never has. He's so mysterious and murky and cantankerous, like a big huge knot that can't be undone, and we hardly know much about him but I do know one thing: he's a man of deep, deep habit. Who's cemented himself firmly into this strange, removed world of flying machines and domes and cages and snakes and it'll be impossible to change him, to crack him.

But it's worth a try.

Suddenly, there's an angry thumping on the front door. We rush out of the kitchen, hearts pounding.

'Police! Open up. Immediately!'

We stare at each other in terror . . .

10
PUNISHMENT
NUMBER ONE

'No, no, no.'

Basti's changed completely again – staring at the front door, shaking his head like he's stuck. Like he was when he was outside, in the middle of the street; a roo in headlights, lost.

'Kicky?' Pin begs. 'Do something.'

'What do I say?' I whisper fiercely to an uncle now clutching my arm in panic.

'Say . . . say you're Lady Holland's niece. From Australia. She's gravely ill –'

'And cannot be disturbed under any circumstances,' I finish calmly for him.

He looks at me, astounded. 'Why yes.' As if I may be of some use after all.

I stride to a front door now shaking with the thumping of police batons. Everyone clusters behind me. Deep breath.

'Could you please be quiet,' I admonish through the wood in my most grown-up of grown-up voices. The batons abruptly stop. 'I am Lady Holland's niece. She is gravely ill and demands absolute silence. And why on earth are you doing whatever you're doing? At such an ungodly hour.'

'Sorry, ma'am. We're just trying to find some . . . intruders . . . in the neighbourhood.'

'Intruders?'

'Of the, er, reptilian variety.'

'I don't know what you're talking about. Have you gone quite mad?'

'Er, yes, ma'am, quite . . . I mean *no*. Of course, no. Nothing to worry about. Apologies. Good evening to you, and give our regards to Lady Holland.'

'Good evening. And please do not disturb us with this commotion ever again. Reptiles, in this neighbourhood? Ridiculous. We're not in the jungles of Rangoon.'

'Yes, ma'am. I mean, no, ma'am. Good evening, ma'am.'

They trudge away. I slam my back hard against the front door in relief.

'Magnificent,' Basti whispers, looking at me afresh, 'quite magnificent, Miss Kick.'

Footsteps return outside. We freeze.

'Ah jist think we should try again with this one,' says a different younger-sounding voice with a Scottish accent. 'There's something about this place . . . would Lady Holland really be in *this* . . . Ah jist don't know . . .'

'Come *on*!' yell the rest of them.

'My tea's waiting . . . it's cheese rarebit.'

'Lucky you, I've got Potato Jane.'

'I've got Tomato Charlotte tonight!'

'Oooooh, Tomato Charlotte,' and off they all go, laughing like it's the funniest joke.

Basti taps his head. 'Did anyone mention feeding time?'

'Yeeeeeeeeeeeees!' Scruff yells.

Basti pushes imperiously through two mirrored doors, turns back to us and winks. We lick our lips, shuffle forward. Food at last!

'I do believe there are some extremely hungry mouths to be fed,' Basti declares.

We smile in anticipation.

The doors snap shut behind Basti with a horrible finality.

Oh. Right. The truth dawns: it's not *our* mouths

he's talking about. Basti is all rusty with other people, yes.

Scruff goes deathly pale, clutches his stomach, whispers, 'I'm going to die, sis, if I don't eat something right now, I mean it,' and falls to the ground.

Bert screams.

I drop to my brother, slapping his cheek. 'Basti!' I cry. 'Quick!'

'I'm busy,' comes the voice from the kitchen.

'This is an emergency.'

'I don't do emergencies. You're on Reptilarium time now, and that means nothing is hurried. It feels like we've been in the midst of a tornado since you lot arrived and now I need some blessed routine, and peace.'

Scruff moans, he's sweaty and pale.

'Scruff's in pain. You *have* to come.'

Deathly silence.

'Food . . .' Scruff moans.

'He needs something to eat *right now*.'

'I do not take to being ordered about. In my day children were seen and not heard. Oh yes, word has travelled about your pranks, Miss Kick.'

'Come here. Now.' It's my Aussie nurse voice. 'I'm getting an ambulance immediately if you don't.'

A blanket of silence falls over the house.

Stand-off.

Bang! The double doors are flung open with a dramatic slap. Uncle Basti emerges wearing a crisp white apron. Behind him is a magnificent, many-tiered trolley crowded with silver trays holding all manner of delicacies.

I venture over, reel back. Nothing for humans, in any way. Splendid porcelain tureens of such things as . . . 'What?'

'Oh, grasshopper legs, fried mouse tails, worm soup.'

Great. Scruff'll be thrilled at all that.

'What about my brother?'

Basti examines the problem. Examines his trolley.

'Hmm. My top-secret Bolivian paste may just do the trick.' He indicates a purple goo piled high in a silver bowl. Scoops up a spoonful, holds it under Scruff's nose. 'Dried spiders,' Basti adds helpfully.

Scruff flurries back in alarm, fully awake now.

'Go on, Master Scruff!' his uncle urges. 'It's a hundred times more effective than chocolate.'

Scruff looks at him dubiously.

'It's good for you.' Basti moves closer, drops his voice. 'Man to man, my boy. It'll put hairs on your chest. Come on.'

Our hearts tighten, tighten at something Dad said to Scruff all the time. I bite my knuckle, bite away tears. Why did Dad never speak of Basti? Why are we really here?

'Daddy used to say that,' Bert ventures. 'Hairs on your chest . . .'

'Sssh, yes, now eat, boy, eat.'

Gamely, gingerly, Scruff dips in a finger. Licks it, makes a horrible face, and swallows. Basti spoons some more into his mouth, quick smart. Scruff gulps. Holds out his tongue for more. More. And more. Until the purple goo is quite, quite gone.

'I bet you feel like a million pounds now. Pay attention to your uncle and you'll go far, young man.'

Scruff springs to attention and gazes ravenously at the rest of the trolley.

Basti's all too happy to oblige. 'Dried mice, crushed ants, pureed cockroaches, grasshoppers. Yes! Grasshoppers. That'll do the trick. You'll have your energy back in no time.'

Scruff lifts up a spindly green leg and with a grin throws it whole into his mouth. And another. Falls into grasshopper-agonies on the floor.

'Right, that's breakfast, lunch and dinner for you, then.' Basti steps breezily over him, slapping his hands at a job well done.

Scruff sits up, giggling. Pulls down his singlet and examines his chest. 'Any sign? Am I a man yet?'

'Oh, we'll toughen you up in no time,' Basti laughs. 'Now come, troops, there's work to be done. You've barely begun the test.' He looks us dubiously up and down. 'The desert, eh?' Shakes his head. 'They breed 'em tough out there, so I've heard. Well, we'll just see about that. Some fortification first.'

Basti picks up a silver spoon, scoops out a lavish portion of orange mash streaked most alarmingly with green and plops it straight into his mouth. Indicates to the rest of us, with a wink. None of us take him up on the offer.

〜

'Hold him, behind the head, like this,' Basti instructs, handing me a glow worm. We're in the Lumen Room, according to a plaque outside its door.

'Quick, I'll just turn off the lights. Now . . . watch!'

We gasp as the animals' skins come thrillingly alive in the dark. Spin around . . . the black painted walls are filled with the creatures . . . hundreds and hundreds of them . . . all softly, magically glowing.

'You could read in here, Miss Kick. I hear you've always got your head in a book – when you're not throwing woomeras at people.'

I turn, laughing, mouth wide. It's magnificent, wondrous.

Basti catches my expression. 'It's my favourite room too, you know.'

'Can I sleep in it?'

'Oh, I've got something else in store for you. Now, to the ladders! Third floor. Green door on the right. Quick!'

Real life's intruding. It's time to ask him about food and clothes and beds as mouths yawn and little bodies slump but Basti's so madly, crazily enthusiastic, sweeping us off as if there's not a second to be wasted, like a big kid with the keys to the secret kingdom and only for a night!

'Quick, my little girlies are hungry!' he cries.

In a lime-green room he coos at four goannas then throws them eight mice in bunches by their tails. 'Don't worry, freshly dead, easy to handle.'

In the room next door he holds a tiny, almost transparent gecko and explains that its tail will detach if it's being chased, it will twist and cartwheel – 'to throw its predator off the scent. This dear little chap is a complete wonder of nature.'

Hang on.

My back prickles up.

Because everything, suddenly, is quiet. Too quiet. Well yes, there's noise: but crucially, no sister-noise.

'Bert?'

No answer.

'Albertina?' Still no answer and it usually makes her come.

I launch myself onto a ladder. 'Come on, everyone, Bert could be wrapped in the coils of a twenty-foot python by now!'

'*This* is why I don't allow children in the house,' Basti says, slipping his gecko reluctantly into his pocket, 'because they most inconveniently get swallowed and eaten and bitten and lost.'

My heart's thudding. Because with Bert something's only ever wrong . . . when she's very, very quiet.

Well well well.

It doesn't take long.

Perdita's cage, of course. The hospital one. Trying her hardest to work out the combination of its tiny padlock, all the while blowing chirpy little kisses to its disgruntled inhabitant. Perdita's crouched at the back, her eyes cool and unmoving, watching her rescuer like it's the last thing she wants in her life.

Basti firmly propels her away. 'Now, what was I saying about not having children in the house?

Perdita is deadly. For everyone here but myself. Please take note, young lady. *Please.* She will not make a good scarf.'

He extracts another snake from a cage near the sink.

'Milking time,' he instructs, 'and this is why you have to be careful in this place. This dear little taipan, as you may know, is the deadliest inland snake in the world. One drop of its venom can kill two hundred men.'

The snake lashes out as Basti attempts to milk its fangs over a glass jar. The powerful tail wraps around his arm, trying to derail him; he wrestles with the reptile and firmly brings it under control, smartly clamping its head over the lip of the lid.

'You're really brave,' Scruff observes.

'Selectively brave, Master Scruff, selectively. And certainly not with things like . . . people. Or buses. Or horns or batons or policemen. Or children.' He shuts his eyes in pain. 'My nerves . . . quite shot, you see. Quite shot indeed. Not good with the world, any more. You may have noticed. Still trying to work it all out.'

'What happened?' I ask.

'Oh, it's a long story.'

'Were you in the war? With Dad?'

'The Great War.' He sighs. 'Indeed I was, Miss Kick.' He puts the snake back in its cage.

'Where?'

'Not the same place. Your father was in Gallipoli, I was in Northern France. It's a toss-up which was worse.'

'What happened to you?'

Basti's silent. He bows his head as if the weight of it is too much to bear.

I come close. 'Please?' I put my arm around his back. He doesn't shrug it off. Faintly, ever so faintly, I can feel him trembling under his velvet coat. I squeeze, ever so slightly. 'Sometimes it's good to talk,' I say softly. 'Dad's always saying that. When we're clogged up . . . with Mum and things.'

Another sigh. The trembling is getting stronger. 'They strapped me to the wheels of a gun carriage, if you must know. A cannon. On a cart. My own people. "Field Punishment Number One," it's called. I was chained to this cart while it was firing. In the middle of a battlefield. Boom, boom . . . the whole thing would lurch, pound, shake . . .'

He's silent, I squeeze him firmer; Bert comes up the other side and puts her arm around him, too.

'I, I couldn't do a thing . . . the sounds, smells, mates getting blown up in front of me, horses

132

screaming, everyone in agony, crying for their mothers, for hours it seemed. Hours and hours.'

'Gosh, what did you do to deserve that?' Scruff asks. 'It must have been something really naughty. Did you steal a car? Like Kick? She took Dad's ute once and drove it into a dam. She's the naughtiest person I know. But now it might be you.'

I'm now giving my brother the Number One Look-of-Death: tonight, bedtime, you'll keep.

'Naughty? Me?' Basti laughs. 'Well, I certainly didn't think so, Master Scruff. But others did. You see, I slipped off to a French village one afternoon. Got lost, as you do. Stupid really, absolutely stupid ... that's what happens when you venture into a world you don't know.'

Bert gives him a squeezy cuddle and he hovers his hand gently over her back.

'The ridiculous thing is, Miss Albertina, that before my bit of silliness I'd been quite the war hero. Oh yes. Everyone in the square here knew about it, they were preparing for a hero's welcome home. You see, I'd dragged four mates from the battlefield under heavy fire, all wounded. Three made it, one didn't. Quite the hero, yes. But then a little sojourn in a French village completely ruined it. Changed my life. So. Now. Everything is much quieter.

Nothing disturbs my little world. It's very peaceful here and the crucial thing is, I am completely in control of it. I always know what's around the corner. No one orders me about, punishes me unfairly, forces me to do anything I don't want to –'

'Except for us!' Scruff reminds him. 'We're here now!'

I give him a swift kick. Basti does not need any reminder at this point as to why his life has suddenly galloped from his control, and I'm worried about that Scottish policeman who may come back. I also now know that this reptilarium has to be kept intact by any means, not just for its reptilian inhabitants but its human one, too. This is a refuge, of the most vital sort, and Basti's sanctuary cannot be destroyed under any circumstances.

Because it would destroy *him*.

'Yes, you lot,' Basti sighs, holding the yellow taipan venom up to the light. 'All I can say is, thank goodness for Charlie Boo. Between Perdita and my butler I don't have a need for anyone else.' He looks down at us, arches an eyebrow. 'Certainly not four children from Woop Woop who are far too . . . smiley . . . for their own good. And who frankly –' he peers in distaste, as if he's only just realised it '– haven't a clue how to dress.'

We gaze at our mishmash of Horatio-clothes . . .
but have nothing else . . . are tired . . . starving.

'My tummy's got a headache,' Pin announces as
if on cue.

Basti looks bewildered.

'Meaning "he's still hungry",' Scruff explains.

'Ahh, food. But no one's dressed properly. And in
this house, one always dresses for dinner. Because
one must.'

We look at each other in despair. Right. Well,
that's that then.

Basti claps his hands. 'But wait, there's an army
of people upstairs, in the attic. They can help!
Of course.'

Our heads turn skyward.

So we're not alone in this place?

My back prickles up again. Bert's coffin's up there
somewhere, and goodness knows what else in this
madly eccentric, endlessly surprising house.

I look back at Basti. Not good with people, yes,
and quite dangerously erratic. Do we want this help
or not?

11

WONDERMENTS

But – wonders! – the rest of them are laughing.

How my lot used to, all the time. The joy's bubbling over as they're heading out the kitchen and gazing up in wonder and chattering about what's next and the sound of it reminds me of home, achingly, how it always made our dad gleeful because he'd always say that when his lion cubs are happy, he's happy. 'So laugh, Billy Lids, laugh!' he'd yell as he tickled us before telling us to scat, git, skedaddle, seize the world, be curious.

I watch them all now bounding madly up the ladders and sailing along the railings, shrieking with delight, higher and higher, grabbing the glee and goodness – my heart, all of a sudden, feels like it's swelling, like a ship's sail caught the wind, bursting with . . . what?

Possibility. Hope.

That this might, actually, work. And it's the first time I've felt like this since we've been here. And maybe, just maybe, I can finally relax. Be a kid again myself.

If we can convince Basti to let us stay (difficult). *If* we can make ourselves indispensable so he'll never give us up (impossible). *If* the Scottish policeman never comes back (unlikely). *If* we can squeeze a Christmas out of our uncle (highly unlikely). But there's nothing I can do right at this point, except follow the glee, surrender the worry, and climb.

'You first, Master Scruff,' Basti urges as we all bunch at a tiny door under the dome. 'They're waiting for you.'

'Who?' Scruff turns sharply.

'Just you wait.'

I can see it in my brother's face – the dawning realisation. New people, up here, does he mean . . . ghosts? Frankenstein's monsters? Some mad scientific experiment? It's awfully quiet in there.

'Ah, are they . . . a-alive?' stutters the kid with sunshine in his soul who soars during daylight but shrinks in terror from the mysteries of the night.

Basti prods him on, mercilessly. 'Clothes, boy. Quick. Dinner demands proper attire.'

Food or dead people, food or dead people – oh, I know my brother, know his stomach. Everyone's watching.

'It's a test,' hisses Bert. 'Don't let us down.'

Test, the magic word.

'I'm going in.'

Bingo. And with a deep breath, Scruff's off.

Silence. We can't hear a thing.

'He's not very good with the dark,' Bert whispers to her uncle. 'Monsters and goblins and all that. He sees them everywhere.'

'Oh dear,' Basti says vaguely. 'Perhaps I shouldn't have –'

'I, on the other hand, am fascinated by ghosts. Are there any here?'

'A multitude, my dear Albertina, a multitude. You will be in your element.'

A shout from above: 'Holy moly!'

That's it, Bert's off, pushing impatiently through us, Pin's quick behind her and I'm not far behind them. We tumble into a space crammed with, well, everything, and I mean *everything*, a kid could want. Holy moly indeed. Billycarts and butterfly nets, dressmaker's dummies and dollies, croquet mallets and cannons and parachutes, pickle jars and balloon baskets, sleds and skis and even an army tent erected alongside a stuffed camel.

'Off you go,' Basti urges. 'This place hasn't been disturbed for years. It's all yours!'

We jump on rocking horses, fence with swords, sing through gas masks and balance on penny-farthing bicycles. Woo-hoo! Scruff topples and lands on Basti, who promptly slams on a tin hat for protection: 'The war was never as, er, bouncy as this, young sir.'

At one stage I'm gazing out a little round window with binoculars, across the vastness of London, as far as I can see. Houses upon houses, streets upon streets, right to the horizon; and all the sounds! A great cram of horns and cars, buses braking and dogs barking, people laughing and chattering as they walk down the street. Usually my world is filled with endless emptiness, space, thrumming silence – and now this. In such a short time. The energetic rush of a mighty metropolis, with its heartbreaking bombing scars of rubble everywhere. It's like the entire city is still suffering from some strange pox; horrible wounds of destruction and hate. What they've all been through. And Horatio told us there are other children in this square who've lost fathers, mothers, just like us. We're not the only ones. I wonder what they're all doing tonight. I look around the room – Scruff swinging like Tarzan on a rope from the ceiling, Bert trying to turn a Union Jack flag into a ballgown, Pin talking earnestly to a stuffed dog that he's instantly christened 'Buccatoo' – Bucket Two. I bet whatever those other kids are doing, it's nothing like this.

Could we possibly live here for good? This city makes me feel very small and lost. I'm a child of the bush, its strong, hurting light is deep in my bones, along with its quiet that's so alive it hums. And now such vast . . . difference. The air tastes sour like it's filled up with dirt and cars and smoke. Even walking on London's hardness feels odd after a lifetime of sand, and mainly in bare feet.

But this is our future now, according to Horatio, under this sky that grazes the rooftops like a giant cow's belly. Because our house scorched by the sun now belongs to someone else. As well as Bucket, my darling dingo girl, but I can't think too much about that. I squeeze my eyes shut on tears. Dad would be appalled if he knew we'd left her behind; he rescued her as a tiny pup from the side of the road, her mother's carcass still warm and all her siblings crushed. 'Keep her close, she'll look after you' – they were the last words he said to me as he hugged us both tight, so tight it hurt, like he never wanted to give us up.

And now I have no one. I'm not quite ready for that. I'm sorry, but it's too horribly soon to be utterly alone in the world, to be entirely responsible for all the big decisions in my family's life let alone my own. What if I get it all wrong? Let the rest of them down? Never get Bucket back? I want independence, yes of course, want to be the chief pirate and the general and the bossy boss, but I want someone to put their arm around me sometimes, too – achingly – and to tell me I'm all right; chin up. I shake my head and laugh at the ridiculousness of it all. I'm just as mixed up as Basti in this place.

I look across at him. Lovingly stroking a glass jar with a stuffed baby croc curled inside. Basti catches my eye.

'This, my friends, is the Reptilarium's very first specimen. Isn't she pretty?'

We gather to him, nod.

Basti's suddenly serious, his face fierce. 'But you must never breathe a word about her. Or me. Or any of this. To anyone. Because as I've said before, it will mean certain . . . fatal . . . calamity.' Goosebumps. 'The solemn family tradition is to protect all that the generations beforehand have – most wondrously – created.' We nod. 'Protect, Not Obliterate. That is our motto.'

'But what does the Reptilarium actually do?' I ask, shifting uncomfortably.

'This esteemed institution was initially a shop on Oxford Street before the authorities shut it down. So my great-grandfather took the operation underground, and moved it here. To his home. Which now protects hundreds of exceedingly rare and valuable reptiles from all manner of barbarians.

'London, you see, is a most extraordinary place. Before the war you could buy anything you desired – cobras from us, lion cubs from Harrods, Egyptian mummies in the East End and medieval manuscripts in the West End. This great city is a world centre for many things, including the underground animal trade. We find them. We rescue them. We breed them if they're rare, to perpetuate the species. The only animal I've ever wilfully held onto is my Perdita –' Basti chuckles fondly '– because, well, she won't go. But there's a whole team of secret helpers, ably coordinated by Mr Boo. Horatio – hopeless – won't step near the place. Petrified of snakes, but good for other purposes. The business arrangements. You see, we repatriate, so to speak. Return whomever we can to their natural habitat. It's why I own a plane.

'So *that*, my dears, is why you have *this*.' He looks around in satisfaction. 'A vast accumulation of centuries of . . . wonderments.' He taps his head. 'Including, somewhere, old clothes.' He smacks his head. 'I quite forgot! My friends will help. They're waiting so patiently for you.'

Four Caddy heads swivel in bewilderment. Nope, quite alone here. Scruff's hand finds mine. Is this the signal for the ghosts?

'Now I must leave you to it,' Basti purrs, rubbing his hands in satisfaction.

Is this how Basti makes sure the Reptilarium will never be obliterated? Will we never emerge from this room?

Bert's having none of it. 'Horatio said Kick needed a dress. She has to start being a proper girl.'

Scruff leaps in. 'I think she's beyond help.'

'Troops,' I warn. They know me. I do not do dresses. Never have. Do not do velvet or lace or silk or satin, do not do 'girl' of any sort.

Basti steps closer, peers. Up and down. Nods slowly, as if he's suddenly got the measure of me. Turns crisply to his nephew. 'My good sir, the philosophy in this establishment is that you can be whomever you want.' Turns to me. 'Madam, I command you to dress like no one else. That is an order. Surprise me. I don't care how. You see, I not only admire the courage to be different – I celebrate it. My creed has always been that one must be their own man, no matter what – er, woman . . . person.' He turns to his other niece. 'Miss Albertina. You, I'm afraid, are beyond help.' He smiles. 'And I wouldn't have you any other way.' With that he disappears through the door.

Leaving us alone.

Me, glowing. Maybe he's not so bad after all. He *gets* me. No one else does. Ever. Especially the horrified succession of governesses and aunts who invariably give up. Not even Dad, who was always scratching his whiskers in bewilderment at the blunt cut hair and trench whistles and cut-off trousers for shorts. 'Gee, Kicketty,' he'd murmured more than once, 'I didn't know young ladies were meant to turn out like *this*.'

'Kick,' Scruff whispers, tugging me, 'apparently we're in a room full of people. Did you know?' He spins. Where? How? Nudges close, his teeth starting to chatter. Trying desperately to be brave, I can feel it. Trying desperately not to think of what happens at two in the morning in a big old house . . . or right now. The attic's deathly quiet. Shadows loom. The place doesn't feel near as inviting all of a sudden.

'W-what's behind that curtain?' Scruff whispers. Hadn't noticed it before. One end of the room is sectioned off by a red velvet curtain. Right. I push past my brother. Don't want to do this. Have to. Peek through.

Scream.

A battalion of . . . of . . . dead people!

No. Can't be. I peer closer. At row upon row of ghostly wax figures dressed in a mishmash of clothes. They're life-sized, frozen, terrifying, and the wall next to them is piled high with long wooden boxes like waiting coffins.

'Eeeeeeeh,' Pin screams.

'Baaasteee!' Scruff cries.

We don't want to be in this place at all; we dash across the attic in horror, smack bang into Basti, who stems the tide and leads us straight back.

'So you've discovered my little friends,' he chuckles. 'Ah, we used to have so much fun.'

'Who's we?'

'Me and – oh, never mind. I was a child. Ancient times. When the Reptilarium shopfront shut down it had an old waxworks above it. Thirty-eight dummies were left behind and they somehow ended up in here.

You'll find Florence Nightingale in there somewhere; Dickens, Queen Victoria, Darwin. A friend and I used to play with them. They were our army, school, family, children . . . ah, the hours spent up here . . . the *fun*.' Basti wistfully fingers a lace collar. 'They're modelling your new wardrobe for you, you know. Off you go!'

And with that, the terror evaporates. It's like suddenly being in a shop and we can buy whatever we want. The four of us thread our way through the figures, marvelling at corsets and crinolines, armour and chain mail, helmets and crowns and daggers and swords.

'Finders keepers.' Basti retreats, smiling. 'Whatever you see is yours. Just make it warm, all right?' He winks at me. 'And singular, Miss Kick.'

'But where are you going?'

'Oh, not too far, don't you worry.'

We look at each other. At the ghostly figures before us. Scruff salutes Queen Victoria; he's got the measure of her now. Bert whips off the queen's tiara. 'Terribly sorry, ma'am; needs must.'

That's it, we're off.

Plundering bowler hats and riding boots, flying caps and feathers, pirate hats and pistols; Livingstone's left with nothing but his britches, we don't dare do that with the monarch but all her jewellery's stripped along with a fur stole. The four of us are piling everything on and flinging it off, parading the room and collapsing with giggles and endlessly attempting new combinations until we're, finally, ready, after what seems like hours – every one of us looking extremely, er . . . *Basti*, I guess. Singular, oh yes.

Scruff's got a pirate thing going on, all buckles and swords and waistcoats and with every weapon imaginable. Berti's . . . well . . . kind of everything, if that's possible, but it works magnificently and it's all in black of course and topped off with three tiaras and an ostrich feather on a turban. Pin's a little Lord Fauntleroy in a cram of velvet and lace (well, we may have played dress-ups on him). And me? Jodhpurs and lace-up boots and a corset and a big white shirt and a nifty leather baseball cap and mirrored sunglasses just like Basti's with only one crack –

Hang on . . . what's that smell?

We look at each other and race through to the next room squealing with excitement. Basti claps his hands at the crazy, mishmashed sight of us.

'Bravo!'

Dressed for dinner, to his liking, at last.

In the centre of the room now stands a red and orange Arabian tent. Four lit candelabras are at its entrance and inside, on a Persian rug, is an enormous jumble of velvet cushions surrounding an array of golden bowls with – what?

The smells!

The most delicious aromas we've ever smelled in our lives. We've never seen anything like it: food that's pink, blue, purple; odd-looking leaves, chocolates in lizard and cobra shapes.

'I promise it's not dried ants, Master Scruff,' Basti declares, busily setting out pewter plates and golden spoons and wine goblets with what looks like cocoa inside them. He's now wearing a velvet jacket the colour of a bright yellow sunflower. On one shoulder is a bearded dragon and on the other a butterfly lizard. When the banquet's set he runs to the corner of the tent and cranks up an organ grinder. 'My most esteemed guests, let the feast commence!'

We run forward, squealing.

'*Now* you look like you belong in this place,' he says. 'Oh yes.'

'Yes,' I laugh, 'and nowhere else.'

'Knocking!' Pin says.

'What?' I say, above all the shrieking and exclaiming.

'Knocking, Kicky. Downstairs.'

We strain for a moment to hear, but the rest of us can't wait, we're ravenous, what the heck, we have to dive in.

'Come on!' Basti urges. 'I can't send you out into the world starving, can I?' He leans in. 'My dears, I guarantee this will make you feel like nothing you've felt before. A most singular and spectacular feast awaits you – everything has been prepared as if you were nothing less than kings and queens of foreign climes!' He takes what looks like a fried grasshopper's leg, throws back his head, pops it in his mouth and shuts his eyes in ecstasy. It's Scruff's cue. He throws a grasshopper leg high in the air and catches it in his mouth, chews, swallows, and his entire body jiggles with delight. He's our tester, it must be good, and he's now closely followed by the rest of us.

Mmmmmmmm indeed.

Everything.

In the middle of her third helping of thistle ice cream Bert yawns the longest, widest yawn we've ever seen on her and falls headfirst into her bowl.

'Good grief!' Basti stares. 'Is *that* what children do nowadays?'

'We need to get her to bed.' I haul her up. 'Er, if she has a bed?'

We look enquiringly at our uncle. The room hushes, this is the big moment. Have we – or have we not – passed the test?

Breaths held.

Basti's face lights up. 'Oh, but you do have a bed, you do! The like of which you've never seen before . . .'

'Hurrah!' From Scruff and I.

'But . . . well . . . do you dare?'

Bert sits straight up as if in a trance. 'Bed . . . bed . . . bed . . .'

'There was knocking, Kicky,' Pin urges, 'rat-tat-tat, tatty-tat!'

'Come on, quick!' Basti exclaims, not hearing him. 'You're exhausted, silly me, I should have seen it. There's not a second to be wasted!'

12

MOST *SINGULAR* SLEEPING ARRANGEMENTS INDEED

Basti, with renewed vigour, pushes across a huge drum on the attic floor.

It's hiding an enormous hole cut into the ground. Our uncle cackles with glee; we peer down. Lo and behold, a twisting silver slide! Down, down it swirls, so far that we can't see where it ends – or what's at the bottom.

'*This* will keep you quiet,' Basti giggles, rubbing his hands in anticipation.

I lurch back, never completely sure with him. 'What will?'

'Master Scruff, for one night, and one night only, your bedroom awaits,' he announces.

It takes Scruff all of two seconds to jump in. 'Wheeeeeeeeeeeeee!' His voice disappears.

A thud.

Silence.

'Is he dead?' Bert asks.

'Possibly,' Basti chirps.

'Come on, Pin.' I drag His Sleepiness onto my knees and hold tight; wherever Scruff is we need to be there too. Basti gives us a savage push.

'AAAAAaaaaaaaaaaaaaaaaaaaaaaaaaaaaaahhh!!!!'

We land in sand.

Red sand, the colour of home. It even smells like home.

I lie back in it, laughing in sheer delight and wonderment; Pin tries to burrow into it, to curl up and sleep. I gaze up, quite forgetting for a moment about a lost brother who may need rescuing. This room is too lovely. The ceiling and walls are painted a tall, sky blue – our sky – with soft white clouds of a summer's day – our clouds. For a precious moment I'm home, alone, without a care in the world.

Bert lands behind us, giggling, and Basti after her, still talking, as if the conversation never stopped.

'I've been preparing this room for my sweet little dragons. It's almost done. The slide's an old remnant from a most glorious childhood. I'd utterly forgotten about it – until now.'

'Did you say dragons?' Scruff, suddenly poking his head from a door.

'Why yes. My baby komodos, Clemmie and Winny. They're waiting for you, in a holding pen next door. They look extremely cuddly but are absolutely fearsome –' Basti notes Scruff's face '– to anyone they don't like. Which I'm sure will not be the case with *you*, young man.'

I wonder for a moment: is he doing this on purpose – to make us leave the Reptilarium of our own accord?

'But where am I sleeping?' Scruff looks around in panic. 'I'm not too good at sharing rooms with scaly, spiky . . . dragons.'

'Oh dear boy, no no no, you're not sleeping in here –' Basti runs across to a double door and flings it wide '– but *here*!'

A bathroom. As big as Scruff's bedroom at home. With a huge bath in the centre that has lion claws for feet.

'Your bed.' Basti sweeps his arm across it. 'Imagine. Pillows, cushions, silk throws – a chamber fit for a king! With two fearsome foot soldiers to protect you at the gate. No goblins or witches or three-headed dogs will *dare* take a bite out of you now.'

'Or ghosts?'

'Well, those one cannot stop no matter how much one tries.' Basti looks distractedly at Scruff's stricken face. 'But I'm sure our friends from the other side won't go near a bath. Too . . . er . . . chilly.'

My brother climbs into his new bed. His face . . . not sure. The rest of us hold our breaths – I don't think beggars can be choosers in this situation and oh dear, this isn't going to work, we're failing the sleeping test at the first hurdle. Perhaps it'll be the orphanage after all. Right now.

'You know what?' Basti says brightly. 'I think we need to find a room right by you for that fanged tiger in our midst.'

'The . . . the . . . what?' Scruff's eyes are wide. Oh brother, please.

'Your *sister*, dear boy. Miss Kick. Terrifying, don't you think? Let's go!'

Scruff laughs with relief. 'I'll take this room!'

Basti has both fists clenched behind his back. 'Excellent. Now as a reward, you may choose a hand. Another test.'

'Left!'

In the centre of Basti's flattened palm is a chocolate with a red aeroplane on it. 'For my fellow chocoholic.' Basti smiles, popping it into Scruff's mouth.

'I'm a choccy-wolic too!' Pin holds out both his palms.

'Well then, young sir, you must also choose a hand.'

'That one. *And* that one.' Everyone laughs as he retrieves a chocolate from each palm, pops one in his mouth and gives the other to me. I hand it to Bert.

'Gee, thanks,' she says, with a look that says you're all right, sis, actually, you're all right.

'Just one more thing, Basti,' Scruff asks. 'Is there an alarm clock?'

'Goodness no, we do not believe in rising early here. This establishment knows only one eight o'clock in a day – or nine, or ten, for that matter.'

'But it's to wake me for my midnight feast that's going to consist of nothing but chocolate! Every single night, at the stroke of twelve!'

A clap on his back. 'A man after my own heart!'

And my smile is wide – because Basti didn't retort that we'd only be here one night; that we'd be out in the morning; which means that maybe, just maybe, everything will be fine.

'The fearsome Kick,' he winks, 'you're next. If you dare.'

I gulp.

There is good reason to.

> DO NOT ENTER UNDER
> ANY CIRCUMSTANCES.
> YOU ARE IN DANGER OF NEVER
> EMERGING IF YOU DO SO.
> YOU HAVE BEEN *WARNED.*

The plaque on my new door. Hmm. Large and to the point.

'Any room but this one,' I whisper. 'Please, don't let it be a saltie.'

'Oh, *much* more exciting than a crocodile!' Basti sorts through a huge pile of keys around his neck. His voice lowers. 'This room is more precious to me than any other. And I'm entrusting it to you, Miss Kick. And young Master Pin, if he cares to join you.'

'I'll protect you, Kicky!' Pin exclaims. 'I'll save you from the knocking.'

Great. Something else to add to the worry list.

'Now, what do you dream of being when you grow up, I wonder? An aviatrix, possibly? An explorer, an adventurer? All three, perhaps?'

'How did you –'

'You're too much like your mad father for your own good. Stubborn, singular, fearless, that wild Caddy streak. Oh, I've been getting master intelligence from various family members over the years. They all seem to say you're very ingenious, practical, a natural leader – but never good at following orders from those in authority. Which makes me think you might be up there with Livingstone and Shackleton one day – but a woman, oh yes!' He looks at me sideways. 'And a rather fierce one at that. Far too outspoken. Kind of glary, but extremely intelligent. Oh yes, terrifying. Which are exactly the qualities one requires in an explor-ix, and master spy. Mata Hari crossed with Lawrence of Arabia, a most formidable mix.'

I'm laughing despite myself.

'Young lady, in your chosen profession, one needs to do a lot of research. And *this* . . . perhaps . . . may be of some help.' He flings the door wide. I squeeze my eyes shut in terror, open them to –

A library!

The most amazing library I've ever seen (all right, the only library I've ever seen, but I've read about them). Every wall's lined with books, reaching to the ceiling; an enormous map of the world is painted on the roof; a huge globe you can spin is in the centre of the room; there are armchairs with bellies grazing the floor; and desks with cameras and sketch pads and paintbrushes on them and there are easels with waiting paper and wooden ladders on railings that slide along the shelves just like the ladders in the main room of the house and so many books that Dad would adore, would devour, would command *I* devour . . .

It's so perfect I want to cry. I breathe in deep the smell of waiting words, paper, stories, lives; could stay here forever, yes!

'Off you go, young lady. Dive in, if you please.'

Nothing could stop me. I spin the globe and loll in the chairs and examine sextants and quadrants, marvel at shells and rocks under glass domes and climb the shelves with the rest of the Caddy troops gleefully, wondrously, alongside me; all the time fingers flitting across books, feeling them, caressing them. Now we're enormous spiders darting across the walls, now we're climbing the Andes and Everest; now we're medieval scholars staring in wonder at illuminations; now circus performers sliding along the runners and scrambling from ornithology to geography by way of mythology, zooming up to the ceiling and leaping down from enormous heights.

Oops.

Ouch. That hurt.

Basti winces from the door. 'You need a landing pad, troops.'

'How do *you* know?' I gasp.

'Oh,' he sighs, 'I was a child once too. Believe it or not. And may even, actually, have done exactly what you're doing right now. I think you should lie down for a moment, Miss Kick. Catch your breath.'

Oh no, too much to gulp in this place. An enormous couch under the window, ten feet long, is perfect to sleep on; Pin at one end, me the other. I spin around with the widest grin: this is grand. Endlessly we can play in here, work out circus routines and have exploring classes and, most lovely of all, read books. All of them. Every single one, I can do it. Dad will be so thrilled!

Would be. Would be thrilled. I bite my lip.

'Er, and me, Basti?' Bert asks, twiddling her hair.

'Aha! I'm saving the best 'til last,' Basti smiles. 'Now I know, Albertina, that you were eyeing those long wooden boxes in the attic – but I thought you may like to consider one other sleeping arrangement first before you fold up like a bat.'

We follow him out. Basti reverently opens a large white door on the same floor as the library. Steps back. Lets us wander inside, absorbing, while he waits; I look back at him, catch his eye, he nods and smiles tight. As if he can't quite bear to venture in himself.

It's a room that's gloriously, glamorously girly. All silk and satin and lace, with floor to ceiling windows overlooking the garden square through silver curtains plunging like foam at a beach. A four-poster bed has matching silver curtains. A mirrored dressing table is crammed with lipsticks and powders. A jewellery box has a tumble of pearls and diamond bracelets. Over a marble fireplace is a portrait of the most beautiful woman in a silver dress, holding a cobra. She has the bluest of eyes rimmed with green. Just like Bert's, like all of ours.

The four of us stand under it, mouths wide. Who?

'My mother,' Basti explains from the door. 'Albertina, in fact. And she loved clothes too, Albertina Number Two. But she was not quite as boisterous and, er, *pointy* as the new version that's crashed into my life.' He shakes his head. 'This is the first time I've opened this door for a very long time.' He pauses. 'Years, actually.'

He's quiet. He smiles across at Bert with something like fondness.

'She'll look after you, Bert. Very well. You'll never be lonely in this room. She'll be with you. It's why nothing must happen to this old house – it looks after quite a lot of us.'

And the current Albertina? Er, Albertina? Calling Number Two?

Hopeless. Barely listening. Because she's just discovered a walk-in closet stuffed with ballgowns and kimonos and coats and hats, most of them in either silver or black. And there's no other way to describe it: Bert is in heaven.

Pin clambers onto the enormous bed with his little bottom poking out.

'Duddle?' he asks expectantly. 'This can fit four, Kicky. Come on, duddle. All of us.'

I smile through tight lips, my heart breaking. Because this is exactly what he says every night, to Dad, at bedtime, has always said ever since he could talk – except he hasn't requested it since Dad left.

'Duddle?' he asks again.

We each have our own bed waiting. We're not wearing pyjamas but we're all suddenly so incredibly weary, I can tell, tired like a huge rake is pulling us down into sleep. We should retreat.

'Of course, little babe.' I lie down beside him and without a word Scruff does the same on his other side. Bert comes over and joins us and little Pin squeals in ecstasy; turning from one to the other to the other and patting each of our faces tenderly, gleefully, as if he can't decide which one is giving him the most delight. We giggle. Safe, warm, snuggly and ready for sleep at last.

Basti quietly closes the door.

Leaving the four of us laughing on his mother's bed, laughing away all the ghosts and the dragons and the snakes, laughing away the policemen and the candles, the cold and the rain and the bomb craters and the dark; and most of all, laughing away the sharpness embedded in each of our chests – that our dad is gone, and is never, ever coming back.

Something none of us can bear to think about properly yet.

Then suddenly, just like that, Bert's asleep, snoring on her back, with her turban and three tiaras still attached.

Followed by Pin, on top of her, spread tummy down on her chest. Gently I remove Bert's turban and roll Pin softly onto his side so as not to wake him up and kiss his dear, plump little cheek. His hand hooks like a crook around my neck and draws me in, as he always does in his sleep. I chuckle. Some things never change, no matter what part of the world we're in or how much we've been through. Softly I free myself.

'So have you got your new life worked out yet, Captain Scruff?' I ask.

'Oooh yes.' He rubs his hands in anticipation. 'Chocolate feast. My room. Midnight. Seven days a week. You ready, sis?'

'Only if you're good, remember,' I tease in exactly Basti's voice. 'No noise! No bouncing! No hats!' My hands clamp in mock-fear over my head.

'Excuse me,' Scruff cackles, 'perfection from now on. From all of us. Guaranteed. We're going to be here for a while yet, Kicky, just leave it to me. Through Christmas at least . . .'

'Perfection? From, er, *you*? Oh no,' I groan. 'Well, that's all of us on the street then. First light. You'll be lucky to last a single night, mister.'

But Scruff's already asleep.

'Knocking –' Pin tosses and turns '– knocking, Kicky, must check.'

I'm too tired to give him another kiss, to soothe him, to do anything but close my eyes at this point. The knocking, the policemen, Christmas preparations, the mystery of Dad's fate, they'll have to wait for now. Exhaustion is dragging through my body, dragging me down into deep, beautiful sleep. I glance at my watch – only five o'clock – but outside it's pitch dark.

Golly. This strange, strange country. I've read about its long winter dark that begins at – horror! – three o'clock. This is London in deepest December after all. The winter solstice, the shortest day of the year. In our desert there'd be searing heat on the longest day of the year, the light blazing deep into the night, endless tossing and turning under our mossie nets and a layer of sweat.

But now this. Utterly still, in silver satin sheets.

13

THE MIDNIGHT GATE

Twelve a.m. Pitch dark. The Reptilarium: deathly quiet.

The Caddy kids: hugely, obscenely awake. Scrambled by all the different time zones we've been hurtling through.

Hang on, someone's missing.

PIN!!!!

Three Caddy kids sit bolt upright.

'The knocking,' I groan. 'He's been banging on about it all night. He's gone to investigate. I just know it.'

Bert clamps on her turban, Scruff grabs his slingshot, we race downstairs. The inner door is wide open. Perdita looks at the three of us wearily as if to say, oh no, not you again. At that very moment a note crashes through the letter flap in the front door. It's addressed to 'The Reptilarium's Newest Inhabitants'. That would be us. I snatch it up.

URGENT!
NO TIME TO LOSE.
Come next door immediately.
I HAVE to see you.
A matter of LIFE and DEATH.
Don't tell ANYONE.
D.

'The candle lady. I bet.'

'Do we dare?'

'What about Pin?'

The front door: locked. No way to open it from the inside – except with a key – which Basti's got around his neck. Stuck. Drat.

'Catch her!' Scruff whispers.

I lift up the letter flap – she's just leaving the front gate. 'Wait!' I cry as loud as I dare.

She stops. Comes running back to the door, leans down. 'Quick,' she whispers, greatly agitated, glancing around. 'Before he finds you.'

'But we're locked in,' Scruff exclaims.

'The scullery window. At the back of the house. The catch is broken, it's always open. Your brother found it. Come on.'

So that's where he is! Phew. The little monkey.

'Crawl through. Drop to the ground. There's an old gate in the garden fence. It leads through to my place. Quick.'

'How do you *know* all this?' Scruff asks.

She looks at him witheringly. 'I was a child once too.'

'But how did you know Basti wouldn't get to the note before us?'

'He's a heavy sleeper and a late riser.'

'Who says?'

'Oh, I know many things. He's a creature of habit. And I also know that children love exploring strange new environments in the dead of night. I took a punt and I was right. Quick, come on, I'll meet you over there. It's easy!'

We race through the Reptilarium, squeeze out the window; it's broken, just as the lady said. Drop to the icy ground. The garden's so still, silent, with a ghostly frost. Blackened and mildewed statues loom all through it; they look like they've been frozen in the middle of play. Spooky.

I glance across at Scruff. He's being brave, trying not to look too close. The moon's full. An owl hoots. Bert squeals. Scruff grabs her hand to stop her waking the entire neighbourhood, to hold onto someone, anyone, even a spiky sister at this point. But where's the gate? The wall's solid with icy ivy; no sign of a gap, no sign that anyone's used it for years. We creep, panicky, along the fence.

'Nope, not here,' Bert declares. 'Maybe it's a trap.'

'Ssssh!' Scruff and I snap.

But she's right. Where *is* the blasted gap? Suddenly, a creaking noise.

Panting. Ivy breaking, snapping; the gate's being worked open from the other side.

'Help,' gasps the neighbour's voice feebly.

We rush.

'Push. From your side. It's been decades . . .'

There it is! We flatten our palms on the wood and shove and with a creaking groan the rotting wood gives way. Plop. Off its hinges, with the three of us on top. And, er, someone underneath.

'Aaaaagh.'

A dreadful quiet.

'Gosh, have we killed her?' Bert whispers in horror.

Before we can find out who she really is? Where our Pinny's gone? Why she was so desperate to avoid the Reptilarium and why she's suddenly changed from all fury and frustration to nice?

We leap away. From the ground: a soft giggling sound. Or it could be a gurgle. Frantically we pull the broken gate aside; two ghostly hands rise up like they're coming from a coffin. 'Help, please.'

Scruff grabs one hand, me the other, Bert pushes from behind, and together we haul our neighbour into a standing position.

'Well, *that* calls for some cocoa!' she says brightly.

Phew. Absolute relief. I can strike 'suspected murder' from the worry book.

'How did Pin find you?' I ask.

'The little sprite was so quick and light he climbed the ivy. Up and over, just like that. I heard him crashing through the backyard and thought I better investigate. He kept going on about knocking or something. Can I keep him? He is rather adorable, you know.'

'That's our boy,' I smile.

'Now quick, come inside before anyone discovers you're missing.' Her face is grave. 'Or more importantly . . . where you've gone.'

We race after the rapidly disappearing flurry of stylishness, Bert leading the way – two kindred spirits. And stop abruptly. Because we're on the doorstep of a glass conservatory. Which you'd think would be filled with greenery but no, it's teapots. Yep. All sizes and shapes, hanging from the ceiling and resting on tables, with the most beautiful pink and red flowers planted in them. This really is the most surprising country. Are all its people like this?

'One of my whims,' the neighbour exclaims breezily. 'Bring on the colour! Especially in the direst months. Come on, through the chandelier room, fast. The neighbours can see you here through the glass roof. Can't have that.'

'But why have you . . . changed?' I ask shyly. 'You were so cross before.'

'I know. And I'm very sorry for it. I calmed down, and had a think. I'd been most rude to the lot of you and I apologise. Temper, temper, it's always getting the better of me.' She taps her head. 'Now, where was I? A fresh start, I think!'

Pin comes racing towards us at that moment with a delighted shriek. I sweep him into my arms. 'You little monkey,' I scold, spinning him around. 'You absolute monkey of monkeys.'

'The nice lady found me, Kicky, just like she found you. She finds all of us! Can we keep her?'

'Well, we'll see about that, young sir.'

We step into a room crowded with chandeliers all across the ceiling, red ones, green, blue.

'An admirer from Venice's Murano glass factory,' the woman says. 'He showered me with gifts. Endlessly. Exhaustingly. All to no avail, I'm afraid, but I did get one very illuminated room out of it. Now, downstairs, quick, to the work room!'

She bounds down to an enormous kitchen, with row upon row of black-and-white photographs pegged on strings stretching the length of the ceiling. Portraits, mainly, and fashion shots. '*This* is my real world.' Her arms sweep across the pictures. 'I'm a fashion photographer. In the war I was travelling across the country photographing the home effort. I was barely here, for six years solid. It's good to be back.'

'Wow,' Bert whispers in awe, roaming among the pictures like she's wandering through sheets on a clothes line. The woman follows us close, holding out her hands in a square, zooming in on our desert faces, freckly hands, matted hair, on our crazy mishmash of attic clothes.

'Delicious. Like four mini Masai warriors playing dress-ups. I'd love to photograph you some day.' Her eyes sweep admiringly down the length of Bert's getup. She lifts up Bert's turban. 'I used to wear this myself,' she laughs, 'but it's so *much* better on you. Just fabulous, madam. What a look. You can direct my photographic tableaux any day.' Turns to me. 'And you're quite beautiful, aren't you? Under all that scowl.' She smoothes my forehead and pulls out a reluctant curl from behind my ear. 'But you don't know it, do you? No.'

I blush. Never blush. But I can feel a creeping red, don't know where to look; have perfected the fierce desert glare over the years and now, quite suddenly, can't do it.

The neighbour lifts my chin. 'Your mother must be very proud,' she says softly. 'All that you do for everyone. I bet you're just like her; endlessly looking out for everyone but yourself. Little Pin here is extremely worried about you, that you're not smiling enough right now. He wants his old Kick back. It's why I thought you might need some rescuing, old girl, some bucking up.'

My eyes shut tight on hot, glittery tears. Cracked by kindness, again! And she's wrong: Mum was so impossibly dainty and stylish and glamorous that I could never be like that, ever; and Dad doesn't need reminding of the loss of the love of his life, which is why I am, ferociously, what I am. Totally different to the way Mum looked, deliberately, in every way.

The woman's staring quizzically, right into me, trying to coax out a smile, which is making me blush even more.

'What's your name?' Scruff saves me. Ever the rescuer.

'Dinda.'

'Well, Dinda,' he says, holding out his hand to her, 'thank you.'

'For what? I haven't done anything – yet.' Dinda puts her arms around me and squeezes as she shakes Scruff's hand.

My chest feels tight, as if it's about to crack. I close my eyes shut on a prickling of tears that won't stop; it's been a long time since a grown-up's approved of me – held me – in affection or anything else.

'Oh yes you have, Dinda,' Scruff nods. 'Yes you have.'

She smiles. Bustles about the kitchen. 'Now, why *are* you next door, exactly? Pray tell.' Her voice is suddenly mock light, breezy, like this is the real reason she needs to chisel us out so determinedly from our new abode. She wants answers.

The atmosphere's changed in an instant. I step away.

'Carrot fudge?' Dinda says hurriedly, trying to

draw me back as she finds a plate of bright orange blocks.

As one we shake our heads.

'Potato fudge?'

Nope.

'One becomes rather ingenious during a war,' she explains apologetically. 'All the rationing and what not.' She's stumbling, grasping for clues, fussing over the sink. Grips it suddenly, turns to me. 'I need to know, Kick. Why on earth are you all next door? With him? After all these years.' She's almost bursting with curiosity.

'Why is it so important?' I snap. Because this woman might be able to do me in with a kind word and a hug – but that doesn't mean I'm going to trust her.

Dinda's almost crying with frustration. 'Because no one has visited Sebastian Caddy for many, many years. Believe me, I know. The neighbours tell me everything. Do you *know* what you're getting into?'

I lick my lips. I do not. Glance around in panic, suddenly not sure who to trust, who to listen to. 'He's our uncle.' I pause. 'Apparently.'

'Who says?' Dinda asks suspiciously.

'Well, Horatio. He visited us.'

'Never heard of him. Did you know him beforehand?'

'N-no. But Basti's got our eyes and –' I shrug, rubbing my forehead; I'm tired, addled.

'Not entirely uncommon. Was your uncle, ah, welcoming?'

'I'm not sure.' I bite my lip. 'I can't say.' Feeling like I'm getting in too deep.

'Why are you really here? Where are your parents? Who's meant to be looking after you? In real life.'

'Mum's dead.'

Dinda gasps a sorry.

'And Dad . . . I . . . we don't know.' The troops gather around me. Bert slips her hand into mine.

'I see. Most mysterious. Singular. Isn't it? You don't know. And Basti – has he been good to you? Has he tried feeding you to the cobra yet?'

Scruff whispers doubtfully, 'Kick . . .', and I know what's going on in his head: a sudden big fat flurry of midnight doubt, fed by tiredness and deadly snakes and mysterious relatives and houses that fold out like magic boxes and contain far too many secrets and a lawyer who didn't want to face his client and a welcome that wasn't a welcome at all and a dad who could be anywhere, and like all of us Scruff doesn't know who to trust any more. Why *are* we here?

'I need to know what on earth you're doing in Basti's house,' Dinda almost shouts in frustration. 'It is *not* a place for children.'

Hang on, is she trying to protect Basti here – or us? I retreat to the basement steps.

'You *are* all right, aren't you? Not frightened? Hurt? Who put you up to this? Not Basti, I know that much.'

'No.' Not him at all – he's the last person who wanted this. 'Why are you asking these questions? Do you *know* our uncle? What's going on?' I suddenly want to run from this house, this street, run to a police station, Claridges, a lawyer, anyone but Horatio, run to Dad, find him, get away from all this; just want stability and normality, Bucket and home.

That's it. I'm off. Closely followed by Scruff. Berti. Pin. Clattering up steps, breaths rattly with panic, racing through a Chinese room, into a bathroom, whoops, wrong way, back to the chandelier room, out a corridor and finally, finally, a front door. Unlocked. Blessedly. Out into the slap of a bitterly cold night –

'Waaaaaiiiiiiit!'

From behind us.

'I knew him as a child.'

As one, we stop.

'A most singular, wonderful, cheeky, infuriating and quite marvellous child . . .'

We turn.

'Who I care about very much.'

A lump in my throat. I do not run.

'I just want to help you. All of you. You, your uncle, your father. We need to get to the bottom of this.'

I look at this woman who called me beautiful. No one's ever called me that. 'Why did you tell us it was a matter of life and death?'

'Because . . . I'm worried, Kick. Because nothing like this – like *you* – has ever happened before. I'm not going to hurt you. Trust me.'

'Why are you so angry with him?'

Dinda sighs a big, huge, grown-up sigh. 'Come on,' she indicates softly, 'back inside,' and I trust her, we all do. Sombrely we file back down to the kitchen. She pours some red wine into a dull silver goblet, then takes down four others and splashes cocoa into them and hands each one out.

'Sometimes, children, there are things that happen between grown-ups –'

'I'm *almost* a grown-up!' I exclaim. 'Shoot away.'

Dinda pulls out another curl from under my ear. Smiles. I raise my hands in mock prayer and Dinda laughs in defeat.

'Yes you are. Almost. The lot of you, I suspect. I think you've been through so much. As have many children around here.'

So. Over four goblets of cocoa we get an awful lot about two neighbours long ago. Who were best friends. Born on the same day. Lived next door to each other, were inseparable. All through their childhood, all through their teenage years, they knew every secret of each other and their families and their houses. 'Basti's may be the Kensington Reptilarium, but mine is the Kensington *Fabu*-larium!'

We all giggle. Yes indeed.

'So what happened?' Scruff asks.

With her fingers Dinda makes a square shape and squints, framing an imaginary photo of my brother's grin. She completely wants to avoid the question – yet again. It's obvious. Nup, I'm not having a bar of it.

'Why aren't you still friends?' I persist.

She drops her hands. Looks straight at me. She's caught. A shadow passes over her face, her smile shuts down. 'Another time, my beautiful desert rose. We're all too tired now. It's one a.m. I need to spirit you back to bed. Silently.'

As if on cue Berti yawns; her head drops, she snaps it up, it drops again.

'Let's get you home.' Dinda gently lifts a sleepy Pin into her arms. 'I have to get you back in one piece. But I must see you all again. Keep an eye on you. I mustn't have you disappearing on me, all right? Don't, please, do that. Now that I've found you. Apologised. Embarked on a mission to make sure you're all right.'

No one laughs.

'Now, if you're ever worried in any way, just climb through the scullery window.' She drops her voice. 'And don't forget. I'm always here.' Dinda puts a blood-red fingertip to her lips. 'And tonight is our little secret. You must never, ever breathe a word of it.'

'He wouldn't hurt us, would he?' Pin asks softly, eyes wide.

'Basti? He's got a face that's incapable of cruelty, don't you think? No, it's not *that* I'm worried about . . . it's –' She murmurs vaguely, stops abruptly. 'Now, my little warriors, off to bed!'

We race back through the garden and climb up through the scullery window; we've never been up so late in our lives. The four of us round the corner and burst into the entrance hall and run smack bang into . . . Uncle Basti.

A face like thunder.

Clutching the keys around his neck.

Shaking with rage.

We gasp in shock.

'*Not* so fast,' he hisses furiously, raising a trembling hand as if he's going to strike us.

14
BUT WHO TO TRUST, WHO?

'What did she tell you? You're *mine*, not hers.'

'We are not yours!' I respond, indignant. 'You don't own any of us. You're nothing like our family, our father. Don't even pretend to be that.'

The air is quiet like it's been stunned.

'We just had a cup of cocoa.' Scruff steps in and shrugs companionably, making me feel very small indeed. 'Dinda said you used to play together, Basti.'

Our uncle draws in his breath. His fists clench.

I'm scared of this new uncle. He's too unpredictable. Maybe the war broke him a bit. This is getting too hard.

Basti suddenly bangs the table that Perdita's cage is on, smashes his hand down so hard that his beloved snake is flung against the bars, hissing wildly. Then he covers his head in his hands as if it's all too much, as if his whole existence is crashing in around him.

Because of us.

Because of our mere being here, mucking everything up, I just know it. And we didn't ask for it anyway, but goodness, everything we've made happen since we arrived! His entire world infiltrated, turned upside down. He lets out an agonised groan of frustration.

'Dinda said she'd love to see us again,' Scruff prattles on, oblivious.

'*Never* mention that woman's name again. Never. Never. NEVER!'

A monstrous fury rings through the house; the reptiles wake, scrabbling and thrashing. We stare in shock. Basti steps back and covers his mouth in anguish; looking at us, looking at his reptiles, as if he had no idea he could have such an effect. And at that, it's as if a great storm has passed. He drops his hand and an enormous weariness comes over him.

'Go to bed,' he sighs, waving us off, and shuffles away with his back to us.

'Why is she called Dinda?' Scruff again, of course, the one who never knows when to stop. Who'll be a detective one day if he puts his head to it.

Basti halts. 'It's short for Lucinda. Which couldn't be pronounced.'

'Who on earth couldn't say Lucinda? It's not that hard.' Bert laughs scornfully.

Basti turns. 'Me, actually.' A pause. 'You Australians are awfully . . . present . . . aren't you? Forward. You've never heard of being seen and not heard, have you? In fact, you've never heard of a lot of things when it comes to correct behaviour. Like abandoning the house that is hosting you – at midnight.' It's said more in defeat then anything else.

We stare at Basti, lost for words and certainly not wanting to dob Pin in – even though he has an alarming habit of going adventuring at odd hours in odd places; we've all fallen victim to it.

Our uncle sighs; it's no use. Oil and water, the lot of us. 'The name Dinda came from me, Albertina. When we were young. And obviously she's used it . . . ever since. Who would have thought.' Something in his voice makes us go very quiet.

Pin steps forward. 'I love you, Uncle Basti.'

He doesn't respond. Just lowers his eyes, as if he's barely heard, and shakes his head as if he's trying to shake the lot of us out.

'Love you,' Pin repeats.

'Off to bed. The lot of you,' Basti says, still without looking.

Pin's dear little face is a picture of dejection. His bottom lip trembles.

I can't bear it. I swoop him up and squeeze as tight as I can, squeezing all my love into him. 'Where's our father?' I fling accusingly.

'I – I don't know.'

'Is he dead? *What do you know?*'

Basti turns. 'Look, I – I . . .' Then he stops. Just stops. Like he can't go on. Comes right up to me. Hovers his hand on my head, a whisper of a touch. 'I can't say anything, Kick, I'm sorry.' He squeezes his eyes shut for a moment then shuffles off.

I feel as if my heart is being pulled with him; I want to cry out, follow.

'Berti-bysies?' Pin entreats, snuggling his hotness into my neck. 'All of us together, Kicky? Like before.'

'Yes, yes,' I cry into my brother's softness. Because it's no use. I stare back at the impossible man who's now disappearing through a door, the man who's running his long-fingered hand through his hair in a way that has something ever so slightly of our father in it, an echo so faint but there, and despite everything I just want to run to him and cuddle him and smell him and cry into him in a way I haven't cried since we got the news of Dad; because I can't let anyone see it, I have to be strong, for all of us.

But I'm seeing Dad everywhere. Anywhere, now. In everything I look at, think of; up there with the moon and the stars. In the sun like tent ropes from heaven piercing the clouds in the sky. At my side in bed as I try to sleep, can't sleep. Smiling when I'm grinning, tutting when I'm frowning; he's everywhere and nowhere; nowhere I *know*. It feels like our life with him was real and proper and right and everything beyond it is not.

I need to re-find a proper life again, for all of us. Need to glean a Christmas, to put things right. A home. Someone who'll look after us, who knows how, who can help us find Dad; get to the bottom of whatever happened.

And Basti's no use.

In the morning, first thing, then. Everything will change. It must. I have to make it. I'm a look-a-philiac, Dad's always saying that, teasing that I always have to poke my head into everything, don't I? Well, tomorrow I start. I've been clogged up with grief for too long, running on empty, stunned; forgetting I love adventuring and finding out more than anything – and it's time to get to the bottom of this. Dinda's right, Dad's disappearance is singular – in a way I don't trust. We're bush-trackers, we've all been taught, and it's time to get those skills into action. To read the land, what's round us, to ask questions and not rest until the answer is found.

Whatever it is.

15

SNARED

I spend a horrid night of tossing and turning in Bert's slippery satin sheets and every time an attempt is made to sneak away a little hand shoots out, or a hot pudgy leg, clamping me down and trapping me tight.

Plus it feels like someone's shifting a huge table right by us. The noise is intruding into my jagged, ragged dreams and the pillow's hurrumphed over my head – urgh!

Still there!

Snapping awake. Hurting sunlight. Gosh. The middle of the day. And there's that shifting-table noise again. In real life.

Aaaaaaaaaagh!

It's a man. Standing right in front of us. Who we've never seen before. Is he from the orphanage? Has it all come to an end, so swift?

This new person in our lives is wearing a crisp black suit and bowler hat and an extremely jolly red bow tie. And he's clearing his throat. Very loudly. So *that's* the scraping noise.

'Miss Kick, I presume? I've been so looking forward to meeting you. Karate has been practised in anticipation.'

'Pardon?' Shaking my head in bewilderment.

The gentleman executes a few karate moves ending with a side kick, then looks at me as if to say, not bad, eh?

'Allow me to introduce myself. My name is Charlie Boo. The Reptilarium's butler and manager. And I do believe it is time to wake.'

Phew! So we're not being bundled out immediately from this place.

'Morning. Nice to meet you. What time is it?' I yawn.

He crisply snaps open a fob watch. 'One-o-nine.'

Good grief! The latest I've ever slept in my life! And Charlie Boo says 'nine' in such a lovely way, it's like cramming four syllables into one, making it such a giggly, wiggly, slippery snake of a word. '*What* time did you say?'

'One-o-*nine*.'

I clap my hands in delight and shake Scruff awake – he has to hear it too.

'Master Ralph, commonly known as Scruff, I do believe.' The butler surveys the rumpled ball of hair and whinge and scowl before him. 'Hmm, yes, utterly appropriate and utterly as expected.' He peers sternly at the littlest Caddy, who's now rubbing his eyes. 'And this, of course, must be Master Phineas.' Prods a stirring Bert. 'And very soon I do believe the legendary Albertina the Younger will be joining us, too. Most pleasing to see her here, as I expected this one in a coffin. Good afternoon to you all.'

We stare in wonder. For once, Scruff is struck dumb. Then he realises what bed he's in; what girly, satiny, frilly hell. In front of a man. I grip his hand tight, trying not to giggle, preventing him from exiting the bed-hell that sleepiness has trapped him in. Finally he breaks free, as if the satin sheets have lice in them.

Quick as a flash, Charlie Boo grabs him by the scruff of his neck (which incidentally is how he got his nickname, because Dad was always doing it).

Scruff yelps.

'Now, first things first. Rules. And I do love a good rule.' The butler raises an eyebrow.

The four of us look doubtful in response. Hate rules. Aren't good at them. Dad's always saying that, and so did every governess we'd had, before they would flee in terror.

'Caddys major, intermediate and minor, your lives are about to change, and change utterly. Troops, sit up *straight!*'

We snap to attention.

'Are. You. Ready?'

Four heads nodding, in absolute silence.

'Rule Number One. You will supply a list of all that is required in this house. For instance, anything you would like to eat. Within reason.' He looks straight at Scruff. 'Yes, even chocolate.' His other eyebrow is raised. '*If*, and only *if*, you're good. Soldiers are meant to be paragons of discipline, as you know. There will be no malarkey in my presence. We're not roaming among wild beasts of the desert now, are we?'

Bert nudges Scruff savagely, trying not to laugh: he's met his match. He pinches her in return. Ow!

'Oh, you are not beyond reproach, either, Miss Albertina. I did see that, you know. You have been let off once and once only. Angels, even fashionably dressed ones, can always have their wings clipped.

Now, take note. The daily routine is as follows. Every day I arrive at seven-o-*nine*, precisely. Yes, you heard me, Miss Kick.' He hovers, jutting his chin out in my direction, daring me to come back at him in some way. I do not. 'After delivering the daily supplies and seeing to your uncle's every need I return to the world outside, to administer to the complicated needs of this august institution from beyond its hallowed walls. Right. Any questions so far?'

'When's the chocolate?'

Charlie Boo raises his eyes to the heavens and shakes his head. 'I will endeavour to take care of your every desire, Master Scruff – as long as it is in the ration book.' Then he leans closer and his accent broadens. 'Now, if you desire anything else – I'm a dab hand at the black market. Years of dealing in reptilian matters, through several owners of this building, have seen to that. All that is required in return is that you arrange for the Australian cricket team to lose the next Ashes series. It's been seven years since they've been played and I've been waiting ever so long. So when it all finally gets underway again I will require a bit of good news. Are we agreed?'

'Not fair!' Scruff laughs.

Charlie Boo straightens. 'Well then, no treats from the sweet end of the ration book for *you*, young man. Are we understood?'

Scruff nods, not sure if he's meant to laugh or protest.

'Now, before I leave, the Master would like it be known that he has rooms you are absolutely forbidden to enter.' He glowers. 'On pain of death. They are marked. And he's extremely busy right now. Which means you have a luxurious amount of time ahead of you. No supervision indeed –'

'Oh.' Scruff's rather liking this new bloke in his life. 'All alone . . .?'

'No supervision at all.' Charlie Boo sighs wistfully. 'No one to ask you to eat your sprouts. Do your times tables. Clear the rubble. Paint the shed. Make your bed – even *sleep* in your bed. Beds, for sleeping in? Surely not. They're for jumping on, aren't they? And magic carpet rides and red Indian tents.'

With a distant smile to each of us Charlie Boo hands out four pieces of paper to write our lists on, and with a wink retreats, as smoothly as velvet, nodding to each of us.

'Good day to you, Miss Thomasina, Master Ralph, Master Phineas, Miss Albertina.'

'Bert!' she insists.

'Albertina,' Charlie Boo says firmly – that will be that. We are silent. 'I do think we are going to get along famously,' he adds, with a grin that suddenly makes him look a century younger.

'What time did you say you arrived again?' I jump in.

'Seven-o-*nine*, Miss . . . Kick.'

'Nine,' I try, cramming all the syllables in; it's like marbles in my mouth. The Caddys laugh.

Charlie Boo smiles triumphantly. 'You'll never get it,' he says, and with that he disappears. Leaving us . . . well, quite alone.

With a resolve to find our father, and change our lives.

'Come on, troops!' I rally. 'Operation Desert Tracker has just commenced.' But as we flit by Bert's window we catch what's outside, and stop. Transfixed. Because it's a world that taunts us, jaggedly, like ragged tin through our hearts. A world full of warmly dressed, rosy-cheeked kids sliding down the icy slope of the square on sledges and throwing snowballs and placing wreaths on doors and laughing hugely, joyously, freely – yes, that most of all.

'Friends,' Pin says, tugging my shirt. 'Please, Kicky. Outside?'

We've never had other children in our lives. So close. Yet so far. I bang the windowsill in frustration. Because it's obvious that the London right outside this house is going all out to have the biggest Christmas celebration in a generation, even if that Christmas is about recycling and ration books and patching things together and making do. But there's a lot to celebrate out there.

Horatio told us how it's been six long years of toy shortages in this land because its factories have been far too busy making guns and tanks. Six long years of squashing down the dreaded 'squander bug' – the urge to be wasteful in any way. Six long years of relatives lost, of Christmas parcels being sent back unopened, of dreaded telegrams on doorsteps. Six long years of windows being blacked out on houses and buses and shops and of no Christmas lights, anywhere, so that the enemy planes couldn't spot them and, of course, six long years of not a single candle in the windows of Campden Hill Square.

A girl and a boy walk cheerily backwards up the hill, pulling at what looks like their reluctant dad. They were lucky. Their family is still intact, we can tell from their faces. It hurts. Their dad's got his eyes closed, it's as if they're about to yell 'surprise'. We crane our heads until the family is swallowed inside a warm, glowing house, a pine tree covered with paper chains at its window, in readiness.

The four of us somehow find each other's palms. A huge roar is in my ears as I watch: it's the roar of the waiting world outside, a vast metropolis, my life. Waiting to be collected, rescued; somewhere else; somewhere vivid and cosy and proper and complete.

'The scullery window,' Scruff whispers, reading my mind. 'Fast.'

'It's been fixed, I bet. Overnight. While we were asleep. There's no other way out. We're trapped here.' I just know it in my bones.

Lo and behold, I'm right.

16
DAD FEELS CLOSE

Starving, but no time to think about it; burying ourselves in the library, trying to find the key – any key – to Dad.

What happened, is he alive, could he possibly be? Does Basti know?

Scruff and Bert are right beside me scouring drawers, opening books, checking under chairs, looking for mysterious letters of instructions or crosses on maps, old family records, something, anything. Turning the room upside down and carefully placing everything back. We're not getting any help from Basti – we have to do this ourselves.

But nothing. Absolutely zero in terms of clues.

'Operation Desert Tracker has to widen its footprint, troops.'

'Okay, what's next?' Scruff asks.

'Basti's polar bear room. His inner sanctum.'

Deep breaths, nods. It'll be tough. It has to be done.

'Hang on,' says Bert, 'where's Pin?'

We look around. Not a sign. Groan. Not *again*. And it's far too quiet, in terms of Pin-noise. Which is terrifying. He's not close.

'Quick!'

Frantically we run through the house – top to bottom – all the rooms we know. More frantically we do it again. *Completely* nowhere. And no gaps to escape from, anywhere. How can a little boy just . . . vanish? Silently. Is he in a stomach of some sort? Been spirited somewhere else? My blood runs cold as I think of Dinda, how she said we must never disappear on her, like she almost expected it. There's so much going on here we don't know about. And the only way out – the scullery window – is well and truly fixed. We scour the house all over again.

'Hang on, what's that?' Scruff whispers.

We're back in the kitchen, the third time around. There is a tiny wooden door in the far corner, behind an armchair. Child-sized, Pin-sized – and slightly ajar.

Bingo.

Dad's slingshot with my name on it is whisked from my pocket. Ammunition? Walnuts from a bowl on the table. Stuffed into pockets, as many as I can. Scruff does the same. Takes out his smaller slingshot from his pocket in readiness. Bert goes to the kitchen drawers and finds a breadknife.

'Ready and armed?' I whisper.

'Proceed.' Bert nods, grim.

Slowly, slowly I push open the door. An almighty creak. We wince. *What* has Pin found?

A passageway. Dark. We can hardly make it out. We creep reluctantly inside. It's cobwebby. Narrow. Damp. Dirty yellowy water drips from rounded bricks above us. Urgh, goodness knows what's in it.

'Eeek!' Scruff squeaks, brushing at his shoulder as something – what? – drops onto it. The tunnel leads under the footpath. How can that be? Where does it end? It's too dark to make out. No torch. Urggh.

The floor slopes – not good. The passage gets narrower – not good either. The air gets chillier like hundreds of ghosts are crammed into this space and screaming silently to be free – definitely not good. My heart feels like it's leaping out of my chest here.

There might be some ancient torture chamber at the end of this, a medieval skull tomb, a pit of snakes, a cage full of lost kids or worse, their skeletons. I want to be anywhere but here and yep, I'm first. Can't let Scruff know my terror. Can't let Bert know because she'll laugh. Don't scream, keep moving, keep calm.

'Do we really have to do this?' my brother moans as if on cue. 'I'm not sure Pin's here.'

'Dad would never forgive us if he is,' I hiss back.

'Leave no stone unturned,' Bert adds, her voice wobbling, 'come on.'

Pardon? Is my little sister actually working with me for once? Well well. This is a first. I grin my thanks in the gloom, she grins back. Scruff pushes on ahead of us in a strop of bravado. Cobwebs like ghostly curtains cling to our faces, we tear them off. As scared as each other and refusing to admit it, any of us. Pushing on, down, down. Weapons poised.

A feeble light ahead, a room, at last.

'Pinny Pin!' Scruff exclaims.

At the saddest, sweetest sight. Our little man. Sitting on an upturned wooden crate, a towel around his neck like a Superman cape and a crooked crown, from the attic no doubt, on his head. In front of an attentive line of moth-eaten china dolls and dusty, ragged clowns and the baby croc in its glass jar and Pin's trusty teddy, Banjo, who's now swamped in a yellowing lace Christening gown, a tin hat and a vast array of military badges. Opened in front of him is Dad's copy of *The Jungle Book*, the one thing from home I'd managed to pack. And he's telling the story – pretending to read – in exactly Dad's voice. Almost word for word because he's learnt it off by heart. We all have, thanks to Dad.

I drop down to him.

'Friends, Kicky!' Pin cries, beaming to see me. 'I found them in the attic. We're at school now. Sssh,' he adds sternly. 'It's story time. The most important bit of the day. You know that.'

'Oh you you *you*!' I laugh through glittery tears. All that panic for a line of teddies!

We glance around at a strange curved room. The walls and ceiling are covered in corrugated iron. Cages for children, my foot. All that's in it are two narrow bunks, a steel table, an old crate and some discarded tins of food and gas masks. Bert tries one on for size, giggling. 'Where are we?'

'You are in what is known as an Anderson Shelter, Miss Albertina,' booms a voice behind us. We shriek.

Charlie Boo.

Looming at the door. With two bright yellow snakes poking curiously and most delicately from his pockets.

'You have chanced upon the shelter that your uncle would retreat to whenever a bombing raid was imminent. The neighbours tried endlessly to get him to the tube station at the start of the London Blitz, banging on his door and checking up on him, trying to lure him to safety, but he wouldn't have a bar of it. He just wouldn't leave the house, to their anguish. Little did they know he was all prepared down here. Quite cosy in fact.'

'What about the neighbours – were they all right?' Bert asks.

'Lucinda next door was never here, thank goodness – she was travelling the length of the country documenting the war effort. She was always terribly worried about Basti but I set her right. She knew he was in good hands. The Bennett-Joneses on the other side, well, they lost everything. Not everyone was as lucky as us.'

'Why did the Germans target the houses?' I ask, horrified.

'To break us, Miss Kick. To kill us. To crush England's spirit and force us to surrender, but they did not. And this locality was heavily targeted because of the concentration of tube stations in it. This room is where I, also, would go if I happened to be in the vicinity. Along with the prized guests of the moment – Perdita, naturally, and a few others. If there was time. Sometimes there wasn't. We were lucky. Very lucky. Someone, I think, was watching over us.'

He glowers over Bert, still in her gas mask, breathing heavily.

'It is *not* a place where young ladies are meant to be. Young ladies – and gentlemen – who do not know how to follow rules. Some. Rooms. Are strictly. Forbidden. Remember? *This* being one of them. Come along at once, the lot of you.'

'But this is my school, Mr Charlie Boo,' Pin says gravely. 'It's story time. These are my friends.' The little boy pushes the man back firmly towards the sloping passage.

'I see. What a shame. Because your uncle has kindly asked me to pop into each one of your deprived little desert mouths . . . one of these . . . when you are found.' On Charlie Boo's palm are four tiny, white, sugary Perditas.

We gasp.

'*If* you're good. Oh yes. So thank you most fulsomely, Master Phineas. For I will now be indulging my good self, and self only. Four times over in fact. Thank you, indeed.'

One of the sweets heads straight for Charlie Boo's lips.

'Friends, it's holidays, school's out!' Pin yells.

We all laugh.

Now. Brother found, sister on side. Everything under control at last.

Back to the task at hand: secret infiltration of Basti's polar bear room. Priority: urgent.

17
A MIRACULOUS FIND

We must wait until Charlie Boo's left for the day because he's far too efficient for his own good.

Then it's quietly, quickly, to the carved door. I open it a sliver. Basti's not there. No idea where he is. The house is quiet. He may be watching, may know exactly what we're doing – but he may not. We'll have to risk it. Pin's on door watch, the rest of us scatter inside. Looking frantically under couches, flipping through books, throwing open drawers, ruffling through papers; looking for anything related to Dad.

'He's coming!' Pin says. 'Up the ladder, from the entrance hall.'

Quick, quick. Nowhere to hide, not four of us. We'll have to go outside, gather around a cage, pretend we're absorbed in its inhabitant. Just as we're going I spy a notebook under an address book. Yellow paper.

My heart thuds.

The yellow paper.

That Dad's last letter was written on.

I love you so much, my little CRAZIES. Not saying which of you is the favourite—Haha. I'll tell you when I see you!

The notebook's empty but I rip off the top pages and stuff them down my shirt. They'll have to be examined. We're on to something. I can feel it, taste it.

Dad's getting closer . . .

'Quick, quick,' Bert urges.

Just in time to gather around the cage of an ambilobe panther chameleon.

'Good grief, Kick, why are you panting?' Basti exclaims.

I clutch my chest, laugh. 'I'm just so overwhelmed, Uncle Basti. At everything. It's all so lovely, amazing. And family. So overwhelmed I think I need a rest . . . in the library.'

'Why, I'll come too. I haven't seen you all day. I need to know what you desert creatures have been up to. A full report, no less.'

Pin goes to joyfully blurt out everything; Scruff scoops him up and whizzes him around into silence.

'The library!' I laugh, my hands crossed at my shoulders.

The yellow pages burning a hole in my chest.

'Who exactly *am* I? Gosh, what a question. And you're all awfully full of them this afternoon, aren't you?' Basti's lying with legs in the air, balancing a fire-belly newt on his feet. 'What peculiar things you ask, you lot. I'm not entirely convinced, you know, that children are raised to be proper children in that desert of yours.'

'Maybe they're *more* like kids over there than they're ever allowed to be here.' Scruff's in full-on teasing mode, on the floor, copying exactly his uncle's position. 'Do you know how to hunt with spears, and climb water towers with bare feet, and dive to the bottom of billabongs and shoot jumping roos at fifty feet?'

'I'm sure I could try,' Basti says witheringly, sitting up and deftly catching the newt in his hands. 'Now, what was the question? Who am I, yes.' He raises an eyebrow at his nephew. 'Young man, my full name is Sebastian Octavio Rollo Caddy, if you must know. And precisely who I am, I fear, is now dictated by the four new specimens who have suddenly appeared in my life. *Childus Australis Desertus* indeed. Whom I did not invite to share my world but who are here nonetheless. Most fulsomely.'

He stands.

'One is a chocoholic, just like yours truly. One, I am convinced, is going to take over my business one day and travel to the rivers of China as well as the jungles of the Amazon because she has it in her blood. One of them will be a world-famous fashion designer because she has quite a spectacular way with clothes, yes indeed.' He stares admiringly at Bert's outfit of the day (which consists mainly of the feathery horse's plumes from a funeral procession). 'And one of them, when he's not disappearing and giving the lot of us heart attacks, just wants to cling to my knees for the rest of his life. Most contradictory and changeable, oh yes. Here, there, all over the place, quite a Caddy trait.' He sighs, staring down at you know who. 'And yes, he'll be clinging forever, I can feel it in my bones.'

The newt is placed on his hat. 'An amalgamation of the lot of you, I do believe, at this point. *That* is how you could describe who I am. Quite swampingly, it seems, right now.'

'But *why* are we here?' I ask in anguish. 'Who sent us?'

'It was your father's wish. I'm sure. Wasn't it?'

I'm silent. Need time alone, to think, need to examine those yellow pages.

'Did you love him?'

A pause, as if Basti's thinking very, very carefully about what to say next. 'As much as anyone can love a brother, Kick.'

'What was your favourite thing about him?' If he doesn't know who our dad was, this will snare him.

'His tall tales, if you must know. His mad, crazy, unbelievable stories that never stopped.'

I'm quiet. It was my favourite thing too. Wrestling anacondas in the Amazon, scaling the Sydney Harbour Bridge, helping pandas to give birth on the slopes of Tibet.

'I'm sorry if I haven't been quite what you expected, Kick,' Basti adds softly. 'I don't believe any of us were prepared for this.'

Everyone's silent. Pin cuddles Basti furiously. Our uncle bends down and picks him up, literally prises him off his leg. 'You know, sometimes in my darkest moments I've wondered if it might be rather interesting to have people around me – family, neighbours, something, anything. I don't know. But you see, it's so overwhelming . . . the change. From what I'm used to. Too much. It's been so long since I've embraced the world.' He looks at us as if he's only just noticed us. 'Temporary, this, isn't it? Yes, yes.'

A blanket of sadness falls over the room. Pin clings tighter still.

'Now hurry off and play . . . or whatever it is children do these days. I'm expecting a shipment of extremely rare hippopotamus worms and there's *much* to be done. They need absolute quiet while they settle. They're quite my favourite animals in the world.'

'Why?'

'Because of where they live.'

'Where's that?'

'Inside the eyelids of hippopotami. And guess what they feed on?'

'What?

'Their tears.' Basti smiles in wonder. 'Can you *believe* it? How beautiful the world can be. Now run along, quick, there's so little time and so much to be done.'

'But – but it's almost Christmas!' Scruff wails, can't contain himself any longer.

The air is jangly with shock. The unmentionable . . . mentioned.

It's too much for Pin; his favourite thing, of course, is thrillingly unmentionable words. 'Christmas! Christmas!' he chants gleefully. Yep, he's off.

'Really? So soon?' Basti murmurs vaguely, looking at his watch. 'Good grief. Well, the sooner it's gone the better. Dreadful time of year. Wouldn't know where to begin. And it's so difficult to get fresh mice . . . must start making contingency plans . . . good riddance to it.' He shuffles off, oblivious, tapping his hat to remind himself.

Pin is suddenly – extremely – still. In shock. Can't even bring himself to say the thrillingly forbidden word any more. Scruff just stares after Basti, speechless. Because he now knows, with absolute certainty, that the closest we'll be getting to Christmas is . . . an extra supply of mice.

I pull the yellow pages from my shirt and hold them high. We need some distraction here, some forgetting. 'Quick, come on. The Lumen Room!'

'Why?' Bert asks.

'We need their light.'

18

SCRUFF TO THE RESCUE

We sneak off to the magical room.

It's Basti's favourite room in the building. It's a risk. It's dark, the worms are asleep.

'We need them to know we're here,' I whisper. 'They glow when they get a fright.'

'But we've got to be quiet,' Bert protests.

I throw up my hands in despair. What to do?

Pin grins wildly. He's got it. He runs crazily around the room, arms flapping wildly, looking a right dill; we're try to stop laughing but it's hard and then wonderfully, magnificently the walls and the ceiling suddenly come alive, with light. Brighter and brighter, an incandescent glow.

It's worked!

I take out the yellow pages, exactly like our dad's last note. Hold them up to the wall, one by one, and gaze through them.

First one, nothing.

Second one, nothing.

Third – ever so faint – something written on it, can't make it out.

'I need a pencil!' I whisper urgently. We all scrabble in pockets. Nothing.

'Hang on, around my neck!' Bert's wearing a silver chain that has a beautifully engraved cylinder on the end of it. 'It might be . . .'

I twist the top of it and slowly, slowly emerges a sliver of a tiny, ingenious, pencil. Trembling, I rub it across the centre of the paper. Trembling, hold it up to the light.

good. Do me proud. Laugh often.
ke me laugh too.
n't wait to hear all of your storie
nd go now and live with someone

Dad's note. His very words. His writing. That convinced us to be here. My heart thuds, my mouth goes dry. But . . . how? What? Who? Is it his hand?

Is it forged? Was he at the Reptilarium? I blink back tears, nodding to all of them, yes, yes, it's Dad's; the note came from here, England, from Basti's room.

'But I don't know what it means,' I wail. 'I don't know.'

'Is he here?'

'Did Daddy really write it?'

'Did Basti? Do they have the same writing . . . brothers and all?'

'Is it a trick?'

'What's going on? Are we safe?'

'Tell us, Kicky, tell us what's happening!'

'I can't work it out.' I stare at three expectant, bewildered faces. Have never felt so helpless in my life.

'Well then,' Scruff says firmly, 'we'll just have to get to the bottom of this.'

I nod. 'But not alert Basti in the process. He's not going to help us.'

'How then?' Bert asks.

'We have to get out of here. Find a way back to Dinda. Ask her some more questions. And Charlie Boo. He could be the key to all this.'

We spend a restless, sleepless night scouring hidden crooks and crannies, trying to find some-thing – anything – in the way of more clues. But nothing. Operation Desert Tracker has to widen its scope. First things first: we have to escape. But how?

⟨⟩

I toss and turn on the couch in the library, too much in my head. And we have to act fast. Dad could be anywhere. Trapped, needing our help.

The crack of dawn. Scruff in full battle mode: armour, sword, American Indian feathered hat, war paint in stripes across cheeks (lipstick from Bert's bedroom).

'You are staring at a tactical genius here,' he announces, waking me up. 'Dad's going to be *so* proud of me. Just you wait.'

He rests his piece of papyrus on an old book, dips a feathered pen into an inkwell, and begins to write. 'Oh Miss K, oh Miss Kicky K,' he chuckles. 'We have to escape from here, right? I've been working on this all night.'

When he's finished he hands the papyrus across with a flourish. 'Madam, the order of the day.'

I take it with a grin, shaking my head. 'Scruff to the rescue, eh?' I murmur in doubt.

Cottage Pie

I smile, nod. Dad's favourite.

Bananas

Because Charlie Boo has told us there are constant rumours some will be arriving in England soon, after several long years of banana-drought, and the entire country's waiting with bated breath.

Chocolate

No escaping that one. This is Scruff after all.

FRIENDS THAT AREN'T FROM THE ATTIC

I look up. 'My masterstoke,' Scruff smiles. 'It'll get us out. I think I know Charlie Boo, I really do. It's a man hunch.'

'Well, boy hero, it's worth a try.'

We race downstairs and leave the order on the kitchen table. Scruff scrawls as an afterthought:

Hip Hip Hooray for Charlie Boo!

Thinks, actually, that's a bit forward for an old butler – I agree, far too obvious. He goes to scrub it out, then decides hang on, why not? In fact, scribbles something else:

XOXO

'The genius-ness! Adulation please,' Scruff commands. 'We'll be out of here in no time.'

'*When* we've got to the bottom of this. And what makes you think Charlie Boo will agree to it? He might just hand over some snakes as our new mates.'

'He hasn't dealt with the Scruffter yet.' He turns to the sheet of papyrus and adds just one thing –

FRIENDS THAT AREN'T FROM THE ATTIC And are not of the reptilian variety

We go back to the library and wait.

And wait.

Charlie Boo must have started work by now.

We hear nothing.

The hours pass . . . the morning firms into day . . . pacing . . . wondering . . . despairing . . . nup, it hasn't worked.

DONG!

The enormous sound of a Chinese gong, summoning us downstairs.

We run.

19
THE END
OF...WHAT?

We race to the entrance hall and are met by the sternest of faces.

Are we in trouble? Pin inches behind me.

Charlie Boo takes out a large cane from behind his back. Holds it up to each of us and assesses, as if he's measuring height and length to give us all a good old whipping, to see how much flesh can be covered by it. I bite my lip. Then he winks. Twirls the stick like a baton. Smiles.

We gasp.

'You have half an hour,' he pronounces, stepping back. 'Half an hour to assemble on this very spot with –' his voice drops, he glares at Scruff '– your very cheeky brother.'

Charlie Boo leans towards the four of us: as one we lean back.

'Hmm. Yes. Lists.'

Scruff smiles weakly.

'Well, well, have I got a request for you.' He rolls up his sleeves. '*If* you choose to accept it.'

Scruff's eyes dart to the door.

'There's no way out,' the butler barks, 'unless I say so. Which I think you've already worked out for yourself, haven't you, young man?'

'Possibly,' Scruff squeaks.

'Right. Caddys major, intermediate and minor. You will proceed to the attic immediately.' We nod, wide-eyed. 'You will find the warmest clothes imaginable. Coats, hats, mittens, Eskimo suits, diving suits, anything that takes your fancy.' He looks specifically at Bert, a dry smile. 'Black, yes, if you so desire.' Peers at Pin. 'Young ruffians from the desert *do* know what mittens are, don't they?'

'Yes!' Pin squeaks but I dread to think of what he imagines a mitten is – and worse, why Charlie Boo is letting us do this.

'Why?' I ask him.

'What's happening?' Bert adds.

'Your uncle's worms – that feed off the tears of hippopotami – are arriving at precisely eleven-twenty-five this morning. They are *extremely* delicate, and need absolute quiet to settle into their new surroundings. Your uncle is concerned that they will not last the distance with so much new – elephantine – disturbance in the house.' Is that a smile in the corner of his lips?

'Ha!' Scruff bursts out.

He gets a withering look. 'I have assured your uncle that I will deal with this matter most effectively. As always. I have not explained to him how. I never explain how. But I would like you all to remain in the attic until eleven o'clock precisely, at which time you will make your way downstairs as silently as possible and meet me in the scullery. At eleven-o-nine exactly.' He raises an eyebrow at me. 'No sooner, no later. Understood?' Flexing the cane. 'I shall not hesitate to use this little beauty, you know, if anyone – *anyone* – steps out of line. I need perfect and absolute and utter . . . obedience. Do you hear me, Master Scruff?'

'Aye aye, captain!' Scruff snaps a salute.

Charlie Boo winks.

'*What* time did you say again?' I ask, grinning.

'Oh, you heard, Miss Kick, you heard.'

Eleven-o-nine precisely. Four kids in the scullery, wrapped up in all manner of warm gear and just about jumping out of their skins with excitement.

Charlie breezes in. 'Come on, you lot,' he urges, his accent growing thicker and coarser by the second as he hurriedly shrugs on his winter coat, unlocks the back door and ushers us through. 'One, two, three, four little monkeys – off you go!'

'Where to?'

'The East End, Master Scruff.'

'Of what?'

'You'll see.'

Quickly we're led through the back garden, too quickly, gazing longingly at Dinda's house but there's no time to call out, to catch her eye; I've got so many questions about disappearances and yellow paper and Basti and Dad but Charlie Boo's striding so fast, no time for a greeting let alone a wave.

The midnight gate's still lying broken on the ground but the butler doesn't notice as he sweeps off to another gate in the back fence, which leads onto a narrow cobbled lane where, waiting for us, purring, is the long black panther car that brought us to the Reptilarium in the first place. Which seems like so long ago.

'In you get,' Charlie Boo sings, then leans down to Scruff. 'Now, let's see if we can find you some friends, young man!'

Scruff grins from ear to ear. Winks at me and mouths 'genius'.

I roll my eyes, groan. Right. Can just see it. Insufferable, from this point.

The car revs impatiently. I hurry inside it but suddenly catch sight of Dinda standing at her back window, a knuckle in her mouth as she stares out at us. I go to call out to her – leave the car again – but Charlie propels me firmly in . . . can't yell . . . too late.

Staring back as the car revs away. She doesn't look happy – she looks worried. Extremely worried. Not a good sign. She's trying to tell me something. To mime something. Can't work it out.

'Wait!' I cry but no one hears in all the excitement – with a roar the car's off.

'Woohooooooo!' Scruff and Bert are shouting at the top of their voices. Pin's clapping his hands.

'Who are these friends?' I ask Charlie Boo above the rabble, staring back.

'Never you mind, Miss Kick.'

'I need to know. Dad would want me to.'

'Don't you worry your little head.'

'Where are you taking us? Where are we going?'

'Just wait and see. Relax. Enjoy yourself. It's about time you did, young lady. Look outside. Soon all the bomb damage will be cleaned up – you're lucky to be seeing London like this. It won't last for long.'

I stare out at half houses, windows blown in, roofs gone.

'If you think this is bad,' Charlie Boo adds, 'wait 'til you see the East End.'

'Of *what*?' Scruff repeats.

'Of London, dear boy. You're in the West at the moment. I'm taking you to the East, where the shipping docks and industrial areas are clustered. A region that's particularly densely populated and because of this was targeted – most obscenely – by Mr Hitler.' He sighs wearily. 'And I, of course, chose to live in the very centre of it. As you do.'

Pin squeals in excitement. Charlie Boo raises an eyebrow and looks knowingly at him.

'If only we'd had Captain Phineas in the war room, I do believe the hostilities would have ended a good deal quicker than they did. Coventry, for one – that mighty city – would have been saved with you on board, I'm quite convinced.'

'I'm the captain!' Pin giggles triumphantly, throwing up his arms.

'Precisely. And you are invincible.' Charlie Boo trails off.

I bite my nails, staring out the window, thinking of Dinda craning her head to follow us, standing on tippy toes, trying to signal something – what? – until we were completely gone from her sight. It was as if she desperately needed to keep track of where we were going, what direction, but couldn't, couldn't . . .

'I mustn't have you disappearing on me, all right? Don't, please, do that.'

. . . as we are sped off to goodness knows what.

20

OUT

We're shocked into silence as the car glides through the damaged heart of the city.

We had no idea it was *this* bad. Entire blocks gone, tube stations boarded up, huge piles of rubble, churches smashed in half – some with only their steeples left. A general layer of dust and decay over everything. No – weariness – that's the word. Like it will take a very long time to put everything right.

Charlie Boo catches my eye. 'Sometimes I like to think, Miss Kick, that the gods and ghosts of this grand place have slipped away from their broken churches, and the glee of them, at finally being free, is all around us. Close your eyes. Can you feel them? You can if you try.'

We all shut our eyes.

'Now open. Look around you. Joy! Yes?'

We laugh. Because he's right. Suddenly the tired-looking, pasty-faced people are gone and all we can see is laughter and smiles and bustling crowds, Christmas trees stacked by shops, holly wreaths on vegetable carts, and kids staring in wonder at one newspaper flyer in particular:

STOP PRESS
BANANAS ON WAY
AT LAST

'Look, Charlie Boo, look!' Scruff's jumping up and down in his seat.

'Indeed. And the Reptilarium will be getting one of the very first bunches. I can guarantee it.' He taps his nose.

The car whizzes around the towering dome of St Paul's Cathedral. It's enormous, beautiful, looming in pale splendour. I've only ever seen it in pictures and read about it, of course, and it looks exactly as I imagined: the breathtaking, beating heart of a mighty city.

'Several of Mr Hitler's bombs struck home but they weren't successful, thank goodness. Our little chapel is extraordinarily stubborn. It's the fifth on the site. London, my dear Caddys, is a most glorious place. You can play in history in this city. Endlessly. Several thousand years of it, layer upon layer. I, for one, have been doing it my entire life. *Most* delightfully.'

'Can we too?' Bert asks.

'Pleeeeeeeeeeeeeeease,' Scruff pleads.

'Of course. When we've got our friends. *With* our friends!'

Pin exclaims joyously.

I say nothing. Don't know what's ahead, what I've got our family into; Dinda's still too much in my mind plus the secret of the yellow notebook. Charlie Boo just smiles at me as if he knows exactly my thinking.

'Well, we'll just have to wait for another shipment of hippopotamus worms, won't we? Now, we've almost arrived. You will be good, won't you?' Everyone nods. 'Albertin-*a*?' Yes, even Bert. He just glares at Scruff as if he's given up. Back to me. 'It'll be okay, Miss Kick. Really. Relax. Enjoy yourself.'

A weak smile.

The car turns down a tiny cobbled side street and lands smack bang in the middle of a cricket match. An old plank of wood is the bat and an oil drum is the wicket and the players are a ragtag collection of kids, all ages, all sizes, and various stages of grubbiness – all cheering madly at the new arrivals.

That would be us.

We stare back at them in shock.

Charlie Boo begins to speak. 'These are –'

But Scruff's already out the door – 'Let's go!' – closely followed by Bert. Dad's been teaching her the perfect spin bowl, been teaching all of us, and she's off. I jump out too, can't resist. Dad said I was the best spinner in the Western Desert and it's time to prove it.

Hang on. Pin.

I go back to retrieve him but no, he's not needing any help. Charlie Boo's turned to him in the absence of anyone else. Our little man's sitting in the car extremely still, and quiet, looking up at the butler in absolute obedience, and awe, and shyness. The butler's face is softening at the sight.

'These are my grandchildren, young man,' he's explaining to him. 'They just keep coming . . . and, er, coming. Their names are Lachie, Ollie, Thea, Linus, Lily, Harry, Zachary, Martin, Ella, Paddy, Lucie, Reuben, Clara, Eddie, Justin, Luc, Charlotte, Cissi, Will and cheeky little Jago – who is not unlike yourself. And they are your new friends.'

Pin's smile cracks wide. 'Friends,' he whispers in wonder, as if he can't quite believe it. He climbs up and gives Charlie Boo a kiss on his papery old cheek.

'Now now, no need to get all gooey on me,' the old man murmurs. Then he holds out his hand and the two of them step carefully from the car. He reaches into his pockets and draws out two bulging handfuls of sweets and throws them high into the air and the kids scramble madly after them. I stand beside him – grinning, forgetting – despite myself. At all of it.

'Told you I was a dab hand at the black market, Miss Kick.' He hands across one last sweet. 'Go on. You're allowed to be a kid too, you know.'

I take it. As the new kids swarm around; like they can't get enough of us. Like they've never seen anything like it. Bush kids. From the upside-down world. Brand new species! Check them out! They're stroking our attic clothes and folding out our rough palms and running their fingers through our sun-blasted hair – 'Feel, feel!' – and asking endless questions about home – 'What does kangaroo taste like? You can eat their tail? Have you really got a dingo as a pet? What's a brumby?' – and they want to know everything about the strange way our school is taught. The one that came after all the governesses. After Dad had completely given up.

'Yes, by radio,' I'm laughing. 'Really.'

'So you could talk to the teacher but couldn't see her? She was *three hours'* drive away?'

'Oh yes.'

'Did you wear a uniform?'

'Nope.'

'So you could be in your pyjamas *all* day?'

'Uh huh.'

'School-of-the-air, we want school-of-the-air!'

'What happens when you're naughty?'

'The teacher speaks to our dad.'

'Oh. That's not good.'

'Was he strict?'

'Well, his voice was. Mr Eager was his name. He had the most smashing ties, apparently, even though we couldn't see him. But we could hear him. And worse – he could hear us. *And* he could get cross. Which was sometimes quite a bit. With us. In particular.'

Everyone laughs, nodding knowingly.

'Come on, six and out, bags first bat!' Scruff's had enough, he's champing at the bit.

'Half an hour, you lot, then tea time,' Charlie Boo declares, surveying the squealy, jumbly mass of kids before him.

I can see it in his face: we're all, instantly, friends, his grand plan has worked. He grins at me, I smile back. Brimming. Surrendering to trust at last, putting my faith in another grown-up besides my dad, and it feels wonderful, liberating. Who would have thought.

'Off you go, Miss Kick. Six and out. I bet your dad played it with you a lot. I have great faith in you holding up the Australian end of things.'

'Where *is* my dad, Charlie?'

'He is where he is.'

My heart beats faster. I stare at him. 'Is he alive?'

'I didn't say that. Did I? I can't say that. But if he is, I know he'll be doing his darndest to find his way back to you. And if he isn't –'

'What can I do?' I cry. 'Anything? Please help us.'

'What can you do?' The old man sighs sadly. 'That I do not know. This war, and the previous one, has done terrible things, to so many people. Talk to your uncle, Miss Kick. Be on his side. He's not your enemy. But now, run off and enjoy what's before you. Quick. We don't have long. Give your sister and brothers an afternoon of happiness, come on.'

At that very moment a cricket ball comes sailing towards me. I catch it in a nifty snap. Scruff, Bert and Pin shout in triumph and, well, that's it, I'm off to the crease.

A huge cheer goes up. A boy comes up to me and claps me on the back. 'Bags you,' he says. 'My team, come on.'

I blush, it's all through my cheeks. He's my age.

He stops, grins. 'What's your name?' he asks.

'Kick,' I say, suddenly shy.

'You're . . . swell,' he says, looking at me, head to toe. 'Just swell.' Steps back.

A smile, right through me, shining me up.

'What's your name?' I ask.

'Linus. And don't you forget it.'

Oh I won't. I throw the ball up and down, grinning for no reason. I won't.

'Lunch time!'

We all run to the house, to the most squished-in meal four kids from a wide brown land have ever had. And just about the best. Cheese soup, rabbit sausage, sultana casserole and yep, that good old carrot fudge again. But it's the best we've ever had because we're surrounded by a scrum of new friends who all want to sit next to us; some on wooden crates and others on a mismatch of chairs and five on the floor behind us and Linus right next to me, he's somehow squished in tight and turfed several out and it's a squealy shouty mess of a feast and none of us would want it any other way.

We're all crammed into the back room of a tiny two-up two-down house – 'two rooms upstairs, two rooms down' – and the dishes are served in a flurry of efficiency by Charlie Boo's robust wife, who we're instructed to call 'Granny Boo', just like everyone else. She lifts the four of us in turn and squeezes us into her powdery folds – of which there are abundantly many – so vigorously that we gasp.

'It's aboot time someone did 'at ter yer,' she hoots in delight, her accent much broader than her husband's.

Bert's in heaven. 'Are you from London too, Granny Boo? You sound so different to our uncle.'

'I'm frae Glesga, lassie, and dinnae ye forget it.'

I can't resist. 'Do you happen to say "nine" just like Charlie?'

Granny Boo looks across at her husband. Whacks him fondly with her tea towel. 'Better. None of this fancy malarkey for the likes of me! Nine nine *NINE*. Aw this mixing in la-di-dah Kensington? Aargh, the daftie, he's forgo'en hoo tae chinwag like a true Scot!' Another whack. 'Now off with the lot of yer, I'm puggled,' and she shoos us away from the table. 'Just in case the bouncy li'l kangaroooooooooooos here are wondering, it means tired out, exhausted. And the rest of 'em hear it a lot!'

We're dragged through the house by a posse of tour guides. It's similar to the Reptilarium, bursting with cages and tanks, except they contain all manner of insects. 'Grandpa Boo calls it the "Kensington Insectarium",' explains Lily. 'It supplies the, er, *needs* of his Reptilarium, if you get my drift.' She taps her nose just like Charlie Boo does.

'I've got a pet dancing cricket!' Harry butts in. 'And Linus has Bolivian cockroaches. We come here every day after school and have races in the bathtub!'

'You can come too,' Linus says to me shyly. I nod.

'And if yer dinnae start behaving yeselves, every single one of them'll be ending up in me cooking pot!' Granny Boo shouts up from the kitchen.

'She's always saying that,' Ella giggles, 'especially when we're naughty. This is our favourite place in the world. We love being here more than *anywhere*.'

'Me too,' Scruff says.

'Toffee apples!' Charlie Boo booms. 'Hurry up, or I'll be bagging the lot of them.'

With an enormous amount of whooping the whole troop of us thunder down the stairs. The entire Insectarium shakes. The neighbours next door bang on the wall.

'Aye, put the broom down, Bertha!' Granny Boo laughs, banging on the wall herself. 'Come and get a toffee apple. Quick!'

The neighbours most certainly do. Seven of them. More kids, more wondrous hair-stroking and gazing at freckles, more explanations about skies never rainy and teachers never seen. And so, after several more hours of playtime involving insect-feeding and charades and cricket and more cricket and ending with the Grand Final Race of the Bolivian cockroaches, Charlie Boo finally, finally calls it a day. His charges need to head home.

Our cheeks are shining, our smiles are so wide they hurt and we're filled to bursting with Granny Boo's food – she's just as amazing as her husband at wringing wonders out of a rationed world ('With just a *wee* bit o' help from me precious black market, thank yer very much!').

Fading light. The world dimming down. The lights of London powering up.

Pin falls asleep as soon as the car starts moving and, as we drive back around the vastness of St Paul's, Scruff smiles hugely, in contentment, like a cat being stroked under its chin. 'Thank you so much, Charlie Boo,' he yawns, then he, too, promptly falls asleep, leaning on the butler's arm. His head slips down. With infinite gentleness Charlie positions him back.

'I just loved today,' Bert says softly, gazing out the window at the array of coats, shoes, hats on all the women walking past. Then her eyes start rolling, her curls nod, and in an instant she, too, is hugely – snoringly – asleep, her face jammed against the car window. She, too, is positioned more comfortably with great expertise.

'Thank you,' I smile gravely.

'Don't give up hoping with your dad, Miss Kick. Just . . . don't.'

I sigh. Shake my head. 'Can you help us, in any way?'

Charlie smiles sadly. 'I'm not sure anyone can.'

I stare out the window. 'I loved today, too. So many new friends . . .'

'That would include my eldest grandson, Linus, wouldn't it?'

I look at Charlie Boo, he looks at me, we both laugh.

'Oh Miss Kick, you're growing up. It's all before you now, believe me. And you may come back, of course, whenever there's a new shipment of hippopotamus worms. I'll make sure that's frequent. You're always welcome. Linus may want to see a dress now and then, of sorts.'

'Oh that could possibly be arranged.'

Charlie Boo ruffles my hair, reaches into his pocket and holds out a cricket ball.

I gasp. 'Take it,' he urges.

'But it's your grandkids'.'

'Believe me, I've got plenty of others.'

'Thank you,' I whisper, eyes shining.

'You deserve it, Miss Bradman. These three are extremely lucky to have you, you know. I'm the eldest of four, just like you. And sometimes you might think that no one ever notices you holding things together, making everything right, watching over everyone and never letting them go. But believe me, they do. Oh they do. We're extremely grateful to have you around, Miss Kick. All of us.'

Well, that's it, I'm brimming once again. Filled up with a glittery melancholy. Just that. My eyes are prickling up. I hold the ball to my lips and breathe it in deep, breathe in the smell of our sun, our sky, our dirt of the cricket pitch at home. 'Why did Dad never tell us about his brother?'

'Weeeell . . .' Charlie's smoothness is suddenly – oddly – rattled. 'I can't tell you, because I don't know myself. All I know is that the Great War was a terrible thing, to a lot of men, a huge shock. Many things about it have never been mentioned by some ever since. They were just too horrific. Some soldiers were very . . . damaged. And they may never have quite recovered. They can end up quite cantankerous and contradictory and fragile. But they mightn't be bad people. They just had bad things done to them.' He smiles, bewildered. 'I do know that the two brothers had a huge falling out, years ago, and sometimes these things can cement – harden – in a way that's terribly sad. For everyone. But I really don't know, Kick –' He stops and shrugs. 'I've never asked. It's a private family matter. Goodness, I'm not usually lost for words, am I?'

'No,' I laugh. 'But *why* were we sent to Basti, of all people?'

'That, dear girl, is something only your uncle can answer.'

'Can we come to you for Christmas Day?'

Charlie Boo looks at me with infinite sadness. 'I respect your uncle very much and would never go against him. In fact, I'm very, very fond of him. And the truth of the matter is, I'd be betraying him if I did that. I could never, ever do that. I'm sorry.'

I bite my lip and stare out the window at the lights of London, so many, so huge, such a cram of people deep into the night; of course I understand, it just . . . hurts. That I can't make everything work for my family, can't make everything magical and right.

It starts to rain and once again water droplets streak down the glass before me in enormous tears, reminding me of the first time we landed in this city. I don't know what to do, what to think, what I want any more. Except for my dad, my darling, darling, dad. Achingly. To put everything right, to put me to sleep, to tell me not to worry.

I'm so tired. Scruff's had us up since the crack of dawn. I rub my eyes, it'll be Christmas soon and still nothing's worked out. I need to cement the ritual, be the father of the troops, get things organised. So much to think about . . .

'Goodnight, Miss Kick.' The butler's arm encircles my shoulders.

I lean in and fall asleep. Vastly. It's so nice to have a strong shoulder to lean on, to surrender to someone else . . .

21
THIS CANNOT BE HAPPENING

I wake, tucked up on the library couch, in the velvety dark of deep night.

But tossing and turning. Freezing yet too tired to get up, get another eiderdown, yet the cold is nagging me, just won't let me sleep. Eventually I leap up, furious, and throw on an extra jumper. Flit by the window.

A thick smoke has dropped over Campden Hill Square, wrapping it up in silence and stillness. It must be a fog. I've read about them. It's so beautiful but lordy, why does everything feel so much worse at night? All the worry that's crowding into my brain, clanging me awake . . .

The horror of an empty Christmas ahead, of our bleak future trapped in this house, the horror of little

Pin's face when he asked, 'Kicky, what's happened to Father Christmas? He's not going to find us this year, is he. Doesn't he like us any more?'

Suddenly, gloriously, it hits me.

If no one else is going to give us a Christmas and welcome Santa into this place, then I have to make it happen myself. Of course! Charlie Boo's right: I'm as close to a parent as our family's now got. They've gone, I have to accept it. I can't replace our parents. I can't make someone else either, I can't force anyone into that. I can't *be* them. But I can be something else, a new thing for my family, someone who makes things happen in ways we don't expect. So. Stop relying on others, stop getting cross at everything, just do it. Sparkle up my siblings' lives and stop waiting for someone, anyone, to make our future right. *I* can do it. I'm from the bush, I've had enough practice. I've spent a lifetime getting by.

Family presents? Obvious. Hundreds of glorious things just waiting in the attic. Wrapping paper? Old newspaper. Up there too. Decorations? Paper chains. Cut-out snowflakes. Ribbons from the shop dummies' clothes. Easy. It'll all be done on Christmas Eve, I'll spend the entire night transforming the Reptilarium and they'll wake up in the morning in shock. It'll be for Scruff and Berti, yes of course, but for dear little Pin most of all.

I fling up the window pane and breathe deep. Life: sorted. 'If you want something done the way you want – then just do it yourself. Don't wait for the light at the end of the tunnel – stride down there and light the blasted thing yourself.' Dad's always telling us that and he's so right.

A wail, like a cat. Next door.

I lean out. Dinda never mentioned she had a pet.

Good grief! Up a tree, at the front of her house, the branches are shaking. There's someone there. She's being robbed!

I lean further out. There's . . . something . . . through the fog . . . balancing on a branch like a tightrope walker with some kind of rope around their neck. They've got a big hump on their back and are making their way, inch by inch, towards a slightly opened bow window on the second floor. The drop below them is enormous – two storeys. The window they're aiming for has a single candle in front of a big pile of gifts, which are wrapped in newspaper with thick black ribbon and bows. The robber wobbles, rights themselves, and creeps closer and closer to the candle. To the very stylish gifts.

The gifts.

Oh no. I almost fall out my own window to get a better look.

Berti?

Bert!

Noooooo! The drop's too far, the branch too narrow, she can't do this. She's not the climber of the family, she's the one who stays inside in all her paleness and gothic splendour and makes hats. It's as if she senses eyes suddenly on her – she wobbles, loses her footing. My heart lurches; on the ground below her are these horribly cruel-looking and hard paving stones that will do terrible things to her little bones, her skull – what to do?

The drop's too big. She'll die. My sister will die. My infuriating sister who I'm always saying I want to wring her neck but no, not at all. Desperately I want to yell 'Berti, back, girl, back!' but it'll break her concentration, she's so unsteady up there but so focused on getting to that window; I'm not sure she'll make it because the branch doesn't look like it'll hold her weight and she'll never haul open the heavy pane by herself and I'm locked inside the Reptilarium, stuck.

Hang on, how did she get out?

I race through the library, banging on doors and scrambling down ladders. 'Scruff! Basti! Pin! Wake up. It's an emergency. Bert's in the tree next door, she's going to fall, can't last much longer. We need to get to her.'

Scruff and Pin come running. 'Basti! Basti!' We all yell. No answer – he must be asleep – can't hear. We've no idea where his bedroom is, which door out of the hundreds in this house.

We stop abruptly by Perdita's cage. Empty, its door wide open.

I groan, 'Noooooooooooooooo.'

Of course . . . the rope around Bert's neck isn't a rope at all. It's a very alive – and very deadly – snake. Her latest fashion item, the scarf she's always wanted, and the new pet she's been continually eyeing off. Her new Bucket. Who won't appreciate being out of its cage, on a wobbly branch, in the freezing cold. Can it get any worse?

No. No it cannot. I love that fierce, funny girl.

Front door: firmly shut. Scullery window: locked. Uncle: vanished.

No way out.

A cold gust of wind suddenly blows through the house. Where's it coming from? There must be another room, an open window . . . but *where*?

'Arrrrgh,' I groan in frustration.

'Kick, over here!' Scruff shouts.

A wooden panel, to the right of us. Opened. A secret entrance in the wall. A disguised door that's been slid across. How on earth she found it . . . one of her nocturnal wanderings looking for ghosts, no doubt.

We race through it. To a tiny study with a narrow window like a castle's. Which is ajar. Just wide enough for Bert's slenderness to squeeze through. We get Pin out but then I try. Scruff. Nup. No good. Head first, shoulders first, feet – but we can't, we're too big, I'm almost tearing off my skin trying to do it but it just won't work, too many bones in the way.

A bloodcurdling scream. As if Bert's just realised the impossibility of the task she's set herself, as if she's completely stuck. We're coming! Pin starts crying on the other side of the window. Scruff and I race back to the entrance hall.

'Ba-sti!' I yell with all my might. 'Bert's gone – she's stuck next door – is going to fall – she's going to die!'

'BAAASTIIIII!' Scruff and I now scream, banging on any door we can find. Where *is* he?

He emerges.

Bewildered, lost, from a vastly deep sleep. 'Wh-what's going on?'

'Bert – Perdi – next door – up the big tree – we've got to get them. Save them. The branch can't hold her.'

Basti's face drains of colour.

From outside, another bloodcurdling scream, as if Bert's moments away from plunging to her death.

'Quick!'

Basti races to the front door fumbling with his keys. So many – which one – he takes them from his neck – hands shaking – finds it but is trembling so much he can't get the key into the lock! He drops them. We groan. Pin starts crying on the other side of the door.

'Come on, come on.' Basti has to start all over again.

'We're running out of time,' Scruff yells in despair. It only makes Basti more fumbly.

'Give them to me.' I grab the keys firmly and go through them, methodically, one by one, just as Dad would – supernaturally calm the scarier a situation gets (whether King Brown on car seat or empty fuel tank in middle of desert: always making things right).

Turn the lock.

'Thank you!' Basti claps me on the shoulder.

But Bert's screaming continuously now, as if she's clinging on by her black-painted fingernails. We rush outside. No time to lose.

Through the thick fog we can just see her now hanging off the window ledge, her pale legs kicking in the empty air, her thin arms clinging on for dear might. Perdita's wrapped in terror around her neck. She's wailing, 'Daddy,' over and over again.

'I'm here, Bert,' I yell, 'I'm coming. Hold on, little sis!'

'Kicky, oh Kicky, help me.'

I race to Dinda's door and thump furiously – no answer – no one home. Try desperately to climb the tree but can't, it's too slippery, damp, smooth; can't get a foothold. Scruff tries too but doesn't get any further, then Pin, darling Pin and he only manages three feet. Scruff and I are both champion bush-climbers, leaping up the water tower in seconds and shimmying up ghost gums, but this is impossible in the fog, the bark's too smooth and slippery, we can't get a grip.

'The fire brigade won't arrive in time,' Scruff cries. 'She can't hold on much longer. She's going to die, Kick!'

One of Bert's hands slips off the windowsill and she dangles sickeningly. Everyone screams. Directly below her is a row of horribly sharp spikes on the wrought iron fence in front of Dinda's house. What to do, what to do?

'I'm coming, Miss Albertina.'

It's Basti.

Scruff, Pin and I turn. Stare. At our uncle. Rolling up his pyjama legs, adjusting his night cap and slipping off his shoes. Spitting in his hands and rubbing them together. The Basti who never goes out. Who can't get a grip on the modern world. Who fails to fit a key in a lock. I gaze up at the enormously tall tree – oh lordy, can't have *two* members of my immediate family crashing to the ground and killing themselves here.

'Basti, you can't –' I want to add that he's far too old for this but don't dare.

Because there's a look of such determination on his face.

'Just watch me, troops.'

He starts to climb the impossibly smooth trunk. In the dark. The damp. Like he's done this his entire life. Like he knows exactly where to place each foot, curling his toes in an expert monkey grip – higher and higher – firm and fast.

The rest of us step back in awe. This, our key-fumbly, sleep-addled uncle. There's only one word for it: miraculous.

'I'm coming, Miss Albertina, just hold on.'

Bert manages to get both sets of fingers back on the window sill but her grip's slipping, she's getting weaker, moaning, she won't be able to hold on much longer. Come on, girl, I close my eyes and pray, come on, just a bit longer, you can do it.

'Basti,' I urge, trying not to panic Bert, 'quick.'

Perdita's still wrapped around Bert's neck, clinging tight – it isn't helping. As fast as Basti's climbing, he won't be fast enough. Bert gurgles – it looks like the snake's now accidentally strangling her in its fright. Basti keeps on climbing, swiftly, surely, as if he's done this a thousand times before.

Which, perhaps, he has.

A new uncle entirely.

But is it enough?

Dinda suddenly appears, walking up the hill with a concert programme under her arm. She takes in the commotion and screams as she sees Bert, who's clinging on for dear life and mewling like a terrified kitten now with her legs flapping in the air.

The scream makes Bert lose her grip again. We all exclaim in horror. She swings her hand up and catches the sill but it's obvious – horribly obvious to all of us – that she won't last much longer.

Basti keeps climbing steadily. Faster, faster,

unfazed by the noise below him. He balances across the long, bending branch as nimbly as a circus performer. Will it hold both their weights? It's not strong enough. It creaks, Bert's grip is slipping, the branch creaks again, Bert's hands are now sliding from the white sill.

'Baaaasti,' I cry. The branch is not going to last, is bending most terribly, is almost gone . . .

Bert loses her grip.

Aaaaaaaargh!

Basti lunges down . . . catches his niece strong . . . the branch snaps.

Both of them come crashing, smashing down, down through the branches, to the horribly hard ground way below them. Bert is cradled tight in her uncle's arms, just missing the horrible spikes.

Thud.

She lands on top of Basti.

Everything is most horribly, silently . . . still.

We all stare, breaths held, at Bert splayed on Basti, a jumble of limbs.

Everything askew. Quiet. Too quiet.

22
KNOTS

Suddenly, miraculously, gloriously – Bert sits up.

We all laugh with enormous relief.

'Why did you do it, you crazy girl?' I'm asking through smiley tears.

She looks at me sheepishly. 'Because I wanted to give us a Christmas, Kicky. Make it happen, for us Caddy kids. Dinda had wrapped some presents. The ones on her windowsill. I looked through the binoculars – they had our names on them. I just wanted to make everything all right. For Pin. For all of us.'

Bert comes over to me and cuddles me tight, so tight it hurts. 'I'm so sorry. For everything. I'm so stupid.'

'No, no. You're glorious . . . inventive . . . kind!' I stroke her beautiful hair, which tonight has several ropes of pearls threaded through it. 'Why do you hate me so much, girl hero?' I murmur.

'Because . . . because Daddy will come back and say he loves you the most. Say you're his favourite because you do everything for us and always make everything right. I just wanted to do something too. That's all. You're always so together, perfect.'

'Oh, pet, no. If only you knew.' It's the name that Mum used to call her, and has never been used since, in fact I'd forgotten it until now.

She sobs, and sobs, in my arms.

'Basti's not moving,' Scruff interrupts.

We all look. I bite my lip. No, not this, not now. He has to be all right.

Gently Dinda drops down to her neighbour. 'Seb, it's Din. Speak to us, come on.'

He looks horribly bruised, there are cuts and scratches on his arms and face; his left ankle looks wonky and wrong.

'We shouldn't shift him –' I bite a nail '– he might have damaged his back.'

Dinda gulps a sob.

'Wake up, Uncle Basti, come on!' Scruff cries impatiently.

Nothing. It can't come to this. We've just found him, he's just saved our sister, we've finally got the uncle we'd dreamt of.

'He's a good man,' Dinda says softly, through tears, 'a good, good man. Everyone in this square knows that. All the old people. They remember him. Tell their kids, their grandkids of the war hero who got lost. How as a little boy he used to climb that tree every day of his life. Once. Long ago . . .' A pause. 'Then one day –'

Wait! He's stirring, ever so slightly, his mouth.

'Dinda, look.'

Pin leaps forward; we go to haul him away but he wraps his arms around Basti's neck. 'He's mine,' he says, cross. 'He's my friend.' The little boy leans down and smacks a kiss on Basti's cheek.

Nothing. So still. So quiet.

Pin kisses him again and gently lifts off his hat.

Basti stirs. Opens one eye. 'Captain!' he reprimands, as his hat almost makes it to Pin's head. 'There's life in the old boy yet.'

We all cheer. Enormous relief, whooshing right through us.

'I'm the captain and I'm invins-iple!' Pin declares as the hat finds its place on its new head.

'Indestructible, more like it.' Basti winces, slowly,

painfully, retrieving what is his and returning it to its rightful place. Everyone laughs. 'First of all, my princess. How is she? Intact?'

Bert laughs. 'Gosh, yes. Absolutely yes. Not quite a ghost yet.'

'As much as you'd like to be, perhaps?'

'Not quite, Basti. I won't be trying that trick again.'

'Excellent!'

Slowly Dinda helps Basti into a sit, checking him over, rubbing his ankle, which is swelling, bruised. Bert steps forward and crushes him in a hug then, what the heck, we all do.

'Ouch!' he says, and we spring back. 'No, keep on doing it,' Basti sighs in defeat, 'but gently. It's been quite some time since that tree was scaled. A little weight may have been gained in the interim.'

One by one we drop back, leaving him holding just Pin. Holding him as if that little boy is the most precious thing in the world right now, as if he's never going to let him go.

'Come on, Dinda, we need to hear more about that little boy who climbed the tree every day of his life,' Scruff jumps in cheekily. 'Why would he do that?'

'Wha-at?' Basti looks alarmed.

Dinda grimaces. 'I was just telling them about you and the tree. To my nursery. Every day. As a kid. The champion tree-climber of the universe. Not only this one but every single tree in Holland Park. Remember?'

Basti's shaking his head in warning but it's not enough. We're urging, 'Come on, come on, tell us!'

'Well, one day the Grand Master Tree-Climber of London decided to do a very grown-up thing. Which shocked everyone in this square. He signed up. To fight. For king and country. Even though he was far, far too young. But he wanted to be a big, brave soldier, the biggest, bravest war hero they'd ever seen. That's what he said to me. It was why he would be going away for a very, very long time. I just didn't know how long, did I?' She looks straight at him; his head is bowed. 'They should know, Seb,' she says gently. 'They *need* to. But big, brave Basti Caddy was just a boy. He lied about his age.'

'Why?' Scruff asks.

'Because he loved his country so much, and felt like it was the most honourable, most exciting thing he could ever do. He didn't want to miss out.'

'I wouldn't either!' Scruff says, eyes shining.

Dinda smiles sadly. 'He somehow slipped through the net. As so many did. And he told his next-door neighbour – who was his very best friend in the world – all about it in utter secrecy. How he was going to come back the biggest, bravest hero in the world, with this enormous row of medals across his chest. That he'd be a general by the end of it – she just had to wait. You see, she was his – how do I say it – girl next door . . .'

A glittery silence. Basti doesn't look up.

'Who loved him very much.' A tear rolls down her cheek. 'Who never stopped loving him, actually.'

Basti shuts his eyes tight.

'Who thought he loved her.'

Everyone is very, very quiet. I put my arms across my uncle's shoulders and hold him, and hold him. Can feel his trembling. I squeeze firmer.

'Oh, you should have seen this one as a kid.' Dinda smiles, composing herself. 'He was a shining boy. With the biggest heart. The one destined for greatness, the whole neighbourhood knew it. The best cricket player, horse rider, the square's conkers champion, Dux, Head Boy of his prep school, the best at . . . *everything*. The golden child who chose me – *me* – to entrust with his secret, beyond anyone else.' A pause. 'I never breathed a word at the time. I wish I had now. Because he came back quite . . . changed.'

Basti doesn't move. Neither does Dinda. What to say? Nothing and everything.

'Look, Kicky!' Pin exclaims, pointing at the window that caused all the trouble in the first place. 'Christmas!'

'That's what I was aiming for,' Bert says quietly. 'For all of us.'

Everyone's now staring up at the magnificently wrapped presents in the window, sitting there so enticingly. Dinda laughs. 'And would you believe it, I've just been waiting for you lot to appear to hand them out. Why don't you come in now? I for one need a stiff drink after all this. Anyone else?'

'Me!' Scruff declares.

'No.' Basti winces, standing painfully.

Dinda reaches across to help him.

'Stop.' He bats her away angrily, still in great pain. 'Leave me alone.' As if he can't bear it. What she's just said, the invitation to her house, everyone listening out here to the perplexing history of his life. Everything changing so fast and Basti not in control of any of it. 'I have to get the children home. It's late,' he barks and limps off painfully into the foggy dark, scooping up a stunned Perdita on the way without a backwards glance.

Just like that.

As if he can't deal with what's just been said, can't respond, can't face it. The truth, the past. And it's been years and years of not being able to face it. What's he afraid of letting in? Why is he so stuck?

We can do nothing but follow. I look back despairingly at Dinda, at her crestfallen, broken face. It's not meant to be like this.

'Goodnight,' I say softly.

She raises a hand in lonely farewell, a picture of sadness as she stares after the man next door; the man, we know now, she has loved her entire life, and has never stopped loving.

Who does not look back.

22
BASTI'S GIFT

Home. Perdita extremely pleased to be back in her cage.

Her face saying it all – she's practically begging us to padlock the door and leave her in peace. For good.

Little Pin won't unwrap himself now from Basti's neck. It's as if his hands have been stuck together with industrial-strength glue. None of his siblings are putting him to sleep tonight – there's someone else in the mix now. The Hero Rescuer of the Universe.

'Come on, sleepy head,' Basti says softly, his old self now that we're safely inside the comfort of his home, with the front door firmly shut on everything else.

The four of us tuck Pin into his bed. His uncle tenderly smoothes his curls, and keeps smoothing, until Pin's finally asleep. Basti finally, delicately, slips his hand from Pin's grip – our brother hasn't let him go since he's been back in his house.

'Now, who'd like a banana?' Basti whispers.

'Pardon?'

'There may well be several waiting downstairs in the kitchen, as we speak. Just for you lot.'

'No!'

'Possibly yes. A contact in Africa sent them in gratitude for rescuing the hippopotamus worms. They're more valuable than gold at this moment – and it just so happens that we have only three of them.'

'Race you!' Scruff cries.

Cue four people thundering down the ladders as fast as they can.

Guess who wins?

Basti.

Of course.

He won't have a bar of having one himself, despite us offering several times over. 'Not interested. Off you go.' Which we most certainly do. 'There are oranges, too.'

And from that point onward the evening degenerates into the most ridiculous silliness – banana-peel hats on heads and orange quarters in mouths and competitions over who's got the most outrageous face – Scruff wins every time, closely followed by Basti. Bert keeps on making orange party hats for every head. Finally, finally, our uncle calls it a night.

But wait, not yet; we mightn't get this chance again for some time, it's a sudden new lightness and we shouldn't waste it. I can feel my notorious bluntness bubbling up. It's meant to stay put but I can't help it . . .

'Why didn't you ever see Dinda any more, Basti, after you got back from the war? If she was such a good friend.'

His face changes in an instant. Whoops.

'Yeah,' now Scruff's onto it too, 'how come?'

'*Please* tell us,' Bert adds, ever the romantic.

Our uncle sighs. And in that long, weary exhalation I get the feeling that this is one of the hardest questions he's ever had to face. And now, perhaps, is the time he has to stop running from it.

'Because I was broken, if you must know.'

He slips a banana peel from his head.

'Just . . . stopped. If that is the word. By everything. And I was too . . . *ashamed* . . . for anyone to see me like that. Especially the girl next door. Who –' He stops, can't go on. I put a hand over his. 'I'd changed, yes. Dinda was right. I was the golden child once, destined to conquer the world. Everyone thought that. My dear, dear parents, my wild older brother who'd already left for Australia, off on all his mad adventures –' he smiles sadly at us '– the teachers at my school, the neighbours, Lord and Lady Holland who were like mentors to me.' He pauses, struggling to go on. 'I came back from the Western Front like a maimed dog. Confused, broken, lost. I couldn't face any of them. An utterly different man, and utterly ashamed of it.'

'Boy,' I correct.

He looks up at me and frowns. 'Yes, boy. You're rather handy to have around, aren't you, Kick? I've come to realise that.'

'But Dinda was waiting for you, Basti, for years and years,' Bert jumps in.

'I wouldn't know. I didn't know. I just assumed Din would find someone else. Someone better, someone whole. Just assumed that she wouldn't want the broken dog who'd changed so much; that it wouldn't be fair on such a beautiful, strong, vivid girl. You see, I couldn't bear for her to look at me any more. Couldn't bear for anyone to look at me. Even now. Couldn't bear to go out and be stared at, to have them all whispering about what I used to be and how everything had changed so ridiculously. The legendary Sebastian Caddy. And then this.' He looks up and shrugs with an utter ruin of a face. 'I couldn't bear to have children – any children – around me. Even now. I'm no role model. I didn't want you to know about me. You didn't need to. I begged my brother not to tell you.'

'Why?' We cry. *Why?*'

'Because I'm ashamed. Of me. Of everything I've become.'

'But you're amazing!' Scruff says.

Our uncle chuckles sadly in disbelief as he lifts the banana peel off his nephew's head. 'It was the Somme, Master Scruff. That's what did it.'

'What happened?'

'Well, if you must know, there'd been a call for the last Christmas post the day before, and I'd missed the mailbag. As you do. But you see –' he pauses, his eyes light up '– I'd found a candle. A beautiful French candle. It smelt of lavender. Imagine that, in the middle of a war zone. A villager must have dropped it in their hurry to escape the oncoming battle and I found it on the ground – too late – but I knew that if I sent it to a certain address in Campden Hill Square, even without a note, the young lady of the house would know exactly who it was from. You know who I'm talking about. The girl who's been loving that candle tradition ever since she was a tot. I *had* to do it. And when I saw that French candle in the dirt I felt like a kid again. It would be our secret signal – and Dinda and I had always had our secret signals. Like that knocking Pin heard on the door, that very first night you were in the house. It was her. I recognised it, from our childhood. She was checking up on you, I think, wanting to find out what was going on.'

I nod, smile. Little Pin was right – he did hear something.

'Now, where was I? The war, yes. I slipped away with my precious candle to the closest village, to find a post office. But on the way I passed these huge pits. They were being dug by some Tommies, which means our own men. The pits were so odd. Large and deep. I couldn't work out what they were for because they were digging them behind us as we marched forward. I hadn't been in the war for very long; had done my one foolhardy act of bravery, saving my mates, and that was about it. Then it suddenly dawned on me –'

'What? What?'

'Those pits being dug were for my own body. In anticipation. For the dead bodies of me and all my friends around me. What did the generals know that we didn't?'

We're silent, horrified.

'I just ran. And ran. And ran.'

I squeeze Basti's hand.

'I still can't explain why.'

'You don't have to.'

'I heard shelling in the distance. Boom, boom. I just ran deep into the night, like a little boy in over his neck, not knowing what he's doing really, just utterly spooked. It was horribly dark. Cloudy. No stars, no moon. Finally I found a barn. Couldn't see clearly. Crept inside, feeling my way in the black. I was so tired, we hadn't slept for days and days, the trenches were full of mud and lice and rats and overflowing toilets. I nestled into a corner of the lovely clean straw and just wanted to sleep and sleep and never wake up. I found a spot next to a great knobbly wall and couldn't make it out but I didn't care, I was so exhausted. Then when I woke I could see exactly what it was that I'd camped up hard against . . .'

I hold him tight, dread what's coming.

'The bodies of men. British men. *My* men. Stacked to the ceiling, to the very top. And all their boots were facing me. That's what I'd been sleeping against the entire night. My own men. And I was next.'

Without a word the three of us cuddle our uncle hard, squeeze him, the tightest we've ever cuddled anyone in our lives.

'Yes, I was just a boy. I realised at that exact moment. And that this great wall before me was what this glorious and glamorous war was really, actually all about. Be careful what you wish for, eh?'

I press my wet cheek to his.

'The next day, well, I posted that candle to Campden Hill Square. And that was the last Dinda ever heard from me. Then I walked back to the battlefield.'

'No!'

'Yes. I had to. For those mates who'd lain beside me all night. For me. But I was punished, of course. Desertion. Despite me heading back to the Front an example had to be made. As it does. And the punishment for that wretched term "desertion", even when it wasn't, was being strapped to the wheels of the gun carriage. For hours and hours. In the middle of the battlefield. I was barely fifteen.' He squeezes my hand. 'It . . . it broke me.'

He's so quiet we can barely hear him now.

'I never recovered. I couldn't have my darling Dinda see me like that. She had to live on gloriously, find a beau, live her life. Not be chained . . . to me.

It was just easier after that to . . . never go out. On the rare occasions I did I just scuttled away if I saw her. Avoided her, wouldn't talk to her, couldn't. I was so ashamed. Then gradually I just stopped stepping into the world. Charlie Boo was here for everything, he'd been here since I was a child and he was a huge help. I didn't answer calls, didn't respond to letters from anyone. Dinda. My brother in Australia. Old neighbours, friends. I can't explain it, it was just easier that way. And eventually, after many years, one by one they all gave up. And now –' he takes a deep breath '– here I am. And always will be. And here *you* are.'

Basti looks at us, bewildered.

'Most . . . fulsomely. Yes.'

He smiles. There is a huge, crushed lifetime in that smile. And in the great balloon of sadness that follows I just know it'll be too cruel to ever force our uncle into visiting his neighbour for a drink, as much as I'd like to; into collecting presents and lighting candles; into Christmas, into anything. Charlie Boo's right. He's broken, oh yes. And on this frazzled evening something is stirring in the Reptilarium, something like forgiving love. And with that, finally, comes understanding.

We shuffle off to bed. It's time, for all of us; we're exhausted.

'One more thing,' Bert says, at her door. 'Did *you* write Dad's letter?'

'Pardon?'

'His last letter, that the policeman gave to us. Telling us to come to the Reptilarium. On the yellow paper. It was in his handwriting.'

Basti looks like he has absolutely no idea what his niece is talking about. 'Well, I do have yellow paper in my notepad, yes, but I'm not sure what you're alluding to here, Albertina.'

It's obvious he doesn't, it's in his face.

'The letter we got,' I say. 'It told us we had to come to you immediately, because you're our uncle. That you'd look after us. It said Dad had vanished, somewhere up north.'

'I have no idea what you're talking about. I received a letter from the War Office, as your father's closest living relative . . .'

'*What?*' I rub my head.

'Tomorrow, troops, tomorrow, we're all so tired now . . .' He waves us off in exhaustion, and shuffles away.

We look at each other. The War Office? Is that really what he said?

Tomorrow can't come soon enough.

24

THE MOST SECRET OF SECRET MISSIONS

The day before Christmas. Minus one degree. Frost outside like held breath.

Four Caddy kids: champing at the bit. Because Basti mentioned the War Office, in the same breath as Dad, and it's blindsided us. *What?* Our father's too old, he was taken from a tree, possibly by a croc . . .

Wasn't he?

But Basti's not up yet and so we must wait. In agony. I'm trying madly to distract, to get all of them making four new hats from bits and bobs from the attic – our Christmas presents to our uncle – but it's hopeless, no one can concentrate.

Finally, a song. Basti's awake, downstairs, checking on his Reptilarium charges. We rush out.

'So the War Office?' I demand.

'And good morning to you, Miss Kick. What about it?'

'Our father. You said last night –'

'I did indeed. Surely you must have known?'

The four of us look blank.

'I thought you knew. The mission. In deepest Borneo. To rescue the Australian prisoners of war from the Japanese.'

'What?' I shake my head in confusion.

'Your father had previous war experience, from all his adventures over the years, and a highly specialised knowledge of the area. He knew that particular region intimately. There was a group of diggers being held there, at a little-known camp, and his assistance was requested. It was a top-secret mission. Hugely important.' Basti sighs. 'And hugely brave, and foolhardy, and ridiculous to accept. But that's my brother. Always has been. As you know. Plus it would have got him out of financial trouble – they were offering a tidy war chest if he helped out.'

'But the note, on yellow paper . . .'

'Yes, yes, you keep on going on about that, don't you? I have no idea what you're talking about. I, being listed as his next of kin, received a telegram from the War Office saying your father was missing in action. I presumed I shouldn't have to do anything about . . . children . . . until I'd received some kind of official notification of, of . . .'

'Death,' I wince.

'Quite, Miss Kick. Then shortly after the telegram arrived I received a handwritten letter from him, along with his hunting knife. It was all a bit of a babble. He was under great stress, saying something about telling you that he was on a croc hunting expedition and that he couldn't say the truth because it was highly secret, official government business. You see, he was spying. To put it plainly. In a combat zone. A huge and most delicate mission. And he loved you all so much because you always made him laugh or something, yet he couldn't say which was his favourite but he'd tell you when he got back. If he did. Sentiments like that. You see, he feared capture. Imminently. And he was correct. Which is why he got a trusted villager to send the letter and his knife. To me. The kid brother who he had a lot of faith in, apparently. To make everything right. Of all things. *Me.*'

'But how did we end up getting everything then?' I yell in anguish, my hands at my head, it doesn't make sense. 'The yellow note was in his handwriting. It was, it was him. What's going on here? What's the truth?'

'I don't know, Kick.'

'You must!'

Basti's face flushes, he raises his voice. 'I would not lie to you. I may do many things – fall short in many ways – but I do not lie.'

A throat being cleared. Behind us. Charlie Boo. He's crept up silently.

'If I may be so bold.'

'Please do, Mr Boo, please do.' My hands are on my hips.

'I read the letter,' says the butler.

Basti gasps.

'You left it on your desk, sir. I thought long and hard about what to do. I, perhaps, saw it differently to you. Four children. Orphaned.'

Scruff cries out in anguish.

'*Possibly* orphaned. You, their closest living relative. In a rather large house. Christmas approaching. As a father, as a grandfather, I found it difficult to bear. A lot of families around us have lost the father of the house. Sometimes, tragically, the mother too. The older brother, the uncle; in some instances whole families have been wiped out. I could go on.'

Basti shuts his eyes in pain, shakes his head.

'So, sir, if I could make a difference to one single family, just one, then by God I was going to.'

'You did what?' Basti asks.

Charlie Boo sails on. 'I did what I thought was best, in the circumstances. You'd kept every one of your brother's letters, despite never responding to them. Every single letter over the years describing exactly what these children were like. Oh, they were scamps all right, but lovable scamps, I could see that. It was like I knew them myself. And they were without a home. Without a family. Yet they had all that here, right in this very building . . . and with respect, sir, I thought it might do you the world of good. Bring you out, perhaps.' The butler lowers his eyes. 'I've known you since you were a baby, Sebastian. Seen you off to war. Seen you change. Most . . . distressingly . . . for those that care for you.' He looks him square in the face. 'I have loved you, sir, your entire life. And I have always wanted what was best for you.'

Basti's fists softly unclench.

'I forged your brother's handwriting. Yes, I did. On your yellow notepaper. And handed it over to Horatio along with the hunting knife. Gave him strict instructions.'

Basti starts to protest, but Charlie Boo talks over the top of him. 'I must say, sir . . . your lawyer was in agreement. He, after all, has known you a long time also. The only thing I said Horatio didn't have to do was come near the house. We all know his pathological aversion to cold-blooded creatures. But he flew across the world, to the place that harbours three of the most deadliest snakes on earth, just for you. And for four children who'd just lost their father. Because he, too, thought it might . . . help.'

Basti shuts his eyes, says nothing.

'Datty, where's my datty?' Pin tugs Charlie Boo's sleeve.

Charlie Boo scoops him up. 'Still lost, my boy, still lost. Deep in the jungles of Borneo. The War Office has been unable to ascertain what exactly went on – where he is.' His voice lowers. 'We have accepted he's gone.'

I can't speak.

'And perhaps you must, too. It's time. All of you.'

A deathly quiet.

'I wish Bucket was here,' Scruff suddenly wails. 'I want Bucket more than anything.'

Basti puts his hand on his nephew's head. 'A long time ago, you know what I wished for, Master Scruff?'

'What?'

'That I could live in the Reptilarium all by myself. That no one would ever stare or laugh at me, no one would ever say, "My, hasn't *he* changed?" I wished that I'd never have to mix with anyone – because I didn't need anyone. So I thought.' He takes Pin from Charlie Boo and holds him high in the air. 'My wish was granted.' Pin's gently lowered to the ground. 'Then you know what? Over the years it became so hard to reverse everything. To say, actually, er, I may have made a mistake here. I don't want to be this person any more, I'd like to stop now. I want to be what I used to be. Except I'd forgotten what that was.'

'But you climbed the tree!' Bert exclaims, and despite everything we all laugh.

Charlie Boo melts away. Snow's now falling outside, coating the world in a blanket of stillness through my glittery eyes. I long to be in it, throwing my first ever snowball. At everyone before me. Basti especially. Cracking him open, bringing out the man who puts bananas on his head and oranges in his mouth, making him laugh and laugh, all of us.

'It's never too late to come outside, Uncle Basti,' I cry, staring out at the blanket of whiteness now shimmering through a wave of wet.

Scruff leaps in: 'Hey, we could start with Chr–'

Basti shakes his head, shakes Pin abruptly from his leg. Places the chameleon on his head and hurries off as if a thousand things have to be done, right now, and he's late, so late; it's too much. Except we know he's not late. For anything.

The doorbell jangles. We all stop. Stare down to the bottom floor.

It jangles again. Insistently.

Who on earth could it be? The four of us run to the windows.

Dinda. Looking incredibly agitated.

Ringing again and again and glancing behind her in panic, then banging on the door with two fists. Urgently. As if the most awful thing has just happened . . .

We race downstairs.

'Quick, quick!' Dinda's panting through the wood. 'I've just overheard, at Lidgate's, the butcher's, in the ration queue –' She takes a breath. 'I ran straight to you. It's the police. They're mounting a big expedition – *tonight* – of all nights. There've been complaints. From that time you stopped the traffic. Revealed yourself, with Perdita. Certain people haven't forgotten. They've put two and two together and they're determined to put an end to it.'

'What?'

'Highly dangerous animals and all that. There are rumours, scare campaigns flying around. Some-where in the neighbourhood. A palace of reptilian indulgence, a public danger. There are people determined, absolutely determined, to shut the Reptilarium down!'

Basti's suddenly behind us, deathly pale, his breath rattly; he opens the door and grabs the doorpost. Dinda clutches him by both shoulders.

'They want you taken away, Seb. As the owner. Want you prosecuted. For keeping highly dangerous animals – and having them escape.'

That was our fault, Basti was right, we've brought him the fatal attention – just as he dreaded.

'And any children in the house –' she looks at the four of us as if she can hardly bear it '– they want them removed. To an . . . an . . . orphanage. Yes.'

We look at each other. An *orphanage*? The Reptilarium dismantled? All the animals gone, sent away, killed. And Uncle Basti – carted off to some institution? With no Charlie Boo to help him, or Perdita, or us for that matter? Living among all manner of people who don't know him, don't understand, care. His worst nightmare. It would kill him.

'What can we do, Dinda?' I cry.

'I don't know.' Dinda bunches a scarf nervously about her throat. 'There's only one tiny chink of light in all this. The person who made the complaint . . .

whoever they are ... apparently doesn't know exactly *which* building in the neighbourhood the Reptilarium is in. They've told the police it can only be found one way. That they've heard it's not too smart-looking, but most importantly, it's always –' she hesitates, looks nervously at Uncle Basti '– dark ... on Christmas Eve ...'

I grab him by both arms. 'The candles. Of course. We *have* to do this, Basti. You must let us. To save you. To save the Reptilarium. To save us.'

He starts backing away.

'The police only have one chance to find the house,' I plead. 'Tonight. When all the candles are lit.'

He shakes his head, just can't contemplate it, it's too much. 'It's a trick,' he yells and Perdita lashes angrily against her cage. 'To lure me, to bring me out. It's just some horrible ploy to get me to light those wretched candles, to force me into doing a Christmas of some sort, to get me changed, to have me dragged into life. All of you!' he roars.

'Basti,' Dinda says, 'it's no trick. You *have* to trust me.' She adds, 'Like you used to.'

'No! No! No!'

'I'd never hurt you. I've only ever wanted what's good for you.' She wedges her foot in the door.

'Come for Christmas, at my house, all of you. There's enough food, presents. I've got the tree, candles, everything. I've always wanted to help, Basti, always. All these years. Every so often I'd knock on your door to check. But you'd never open it. I never gave up. Always hoped. It's why I've never looked at anyone el–'

Basti pushes her foot away and slams the door.

In Dinda's face.

We flinch.

In the most horrible, deflated stillness. Of a house in shock. On Christmas Eve. The most awful Christmas Eve of our lives.

Scruff looks at his uncle, man to man. 'It's not a trick,' he says.

Basti just glares at him. 'Let me do Christmas how *I* want to do Christmas. *My* way. Let me live my life the way I want!'

He storms off.

25

WHAT BUSH KIDS DO

The door of the polar bear room: slammed.

Basti's gone. Disappeared. And that's one door that won't be opening anytime soon. We slump with our backs against the front door. It's hopeless. He'll never come out. So much for four half-made Christmas hats or anything else.

'I don't want to go to an orphanage, Kick,' Scruff cries. 'I hate gruel. And they'll never let me put sugar in it.'

I look at him. All of them. Right. Up to me to mend this.

Open our door. Dinda's just disappearing, her door's closing –

'Wait!' I shout, running out, three Caddys behind

me. The door slams, as if she's completely given up on the Reptilarium and its impossible knot of a family.

'I can help,' I say loudly, right outside her house.

The door stays resolutely shut.

'I know exactly what to do. To fix everything.'

Still shut. One last chance. 'Dinda, we know why Basti never speaks to you. I want to help. I know how.'

The door opens. A sliver of a crack. Dinda's eyes are red from crying.

'I can make this work,' I plead.

'Please, Princess Dindi.' Pin holds up his hands in prayer.

A hint of a smile.

'We're going to fix this,' I say, firm. 'Whatever it takes. Because we have to. Because it was our fault.'

'Whatever it takes,' Scruff repeats, looking doubtfully at me.

'So, Miss Desert Rose, what do you propose?'

I lick my lips. Glance around at the other houses in the square. 'We have to hide the Reptilarium among all the others. Just like that refuge was hidden once. We have to put candles all through it whether Basti likes it or not.' A deep breath. 'And the big task: we have to tidy it up.' Another deep breath. 'And then convince him to have a Christmas.'

'A few trifles,' Dinda laughs in hopelessness. 'Anything else?'

'Yes. We have to make him be friends with you.'

'Right. All that, in a day.'

I nod firm. 'Yep. My dad says you never get anything done unless you give it a try. So just do it.'

Dinda looks dubiously at the Reptilarium then dubiously at us.

'Caddys to the rescue!' Bert throws up her arms.

It's my sign. 'Troops, action stations!' I command before Dinda can talk any of us out of it. 'Girl hero, you ready?'

'Aye aye, captain.'

'Boy heroes?'

'Aye aye, captain!'

Swiftly before me, in a line, are three perfect salutes. I look our reluctant neighbour straight in the eye and wink. 'We can do it, Dinda. And do you know why? Because we're from the bush!'

Two minutes later. Four kids from the desert plus one very glamorous photographer standing on a snowy footpath of London's Campden Hill Square, staring up at a magical but decidedly neglected building called the Kensington Reptilarium. With a plan to transform it. In a single day. On Christmas Eve. Are we mad? Yes. Barely a month ago, who would have thought that any of them would be doing this?

'Oh my, it's a task.' Dinda's shaking her head with the sheer, crushing hopelessness of it. 'We'd need a frightfully large amount of people. And we only have today . . .'

'Actually, we only have four hours, until it gets dark,' Scruff says, looking at his watch. 'That's about three p.m., isn't it? This being London and all.'

'Steady on, mister,' Dinda smiles, then sighs. 'But it's today of all days. With the last-minute shopping to do, trees to finish off, presents to wrap. Who's got the time? Anyone?'

I look at her. I look at all of them. 'Excuse me, but where's our spirit of the Blitz, troops? You Brits won the war on it, Dinda. Well, we just need to see it. Here. Now. Again. It's legendary. Give me half an hour. I'll get them out. You told us that Basti was really respected in this square. That lots of the older people still remember him fondly. The little boy who climbed trees, the rescuer of his mates, the war hero, actually, despite what he thinks. He can't be taken away now, he can't be locked up. We *have* to save him.'

And off I set, just like that, striding away determined to the nearest house.

Rap loudly.

A gentleman answers. He's in the throes of gluing paper chains together, a huge string is wrapped around his neck. I explain. His face softens. 'Sebastian Caddy? Why of course. My father used to play with him all the time. Spoke of him extremely fondly.' He unwraps himself from the chains. 'What do you want me to do?'

Bert catches it all. Heads off to another house. Scruff strides away with Pin. Each with one goal: to save Basti, save the Reptilarium, before dark.

Because we're from the bush. And we're Dad's kids. And we get things done, we make them right.

Half an hour later. Campden Hill Square. A huge group of people heading out their doors into the glittery cold of Christmas Eve – it's just stopped snowing, the world's twinkly and white. Every one of them cluttered up with buckets and ladders and brooms and brushes; old people, young people, tall women, short men, dogs and children and people who've never before met.

Heading to? The Kensington Reptilarium, of course.

And over the next couple of hours, in what little daylight London's got left, everyone works, and works, and works. Everyone in the square, on December the 24th, summoning that renowned spirit of the Blitz. To save the man inside the shabbiest house in their midst. The one who they've all heard about or remember. The man who saved four mates once – and sent a candle back to this very square from the Western Front. Aged just fifteen years. And then returned to the thick of battle. Once again, for his mates.

And was punished most savagely for it.

'Come on, Basti,' I plead at the polar bear door. 'Come out, have a look.'

'No!' comes the muffled cry. 'Leave me alone.'

'I'll give you half my Cadbury's ration chocolate,' Scruff entreats. 'It's one of my all-time favourites . . . and yours. And it's not given away lightly. As you well know.'

'No.'

A pause. 'I'll give you the whole lot. This is some sacrifice here.'

'*No.*'

'Basti! Basti! Cuddle?' Pin begs.

Hesitation. Then, 'No,' quiet, from the other side.

'Please, Basti,' Pin persists, 'I love you.'

Silence.

Then the captain does something none of us hear very much: he cries a wail of complete abandonment.

I look at Scruff, at Bert, my heart breaking. Because it sounds like Pin's weeping not just for Basti but for Dad too. He's well and truly gone, we know that, he's never coming back and it's hit Pin at last and it's all, finally, pouring out. Our little brother gets it. Finally. He's growing up.

Look.

The polar bear door, opening a sliver.

A velvet cap peeking out – the one Bert's been trying to get her hands on the entire time we've been in this place. Two bushy eyebrows. Two most concerned eyes. The hat leans down, right at Pin-level, and jiggles.

Jiggles again, most enticingly.

Pin giggles despite himself and gently lifts the cap off its rightful head and places it triumphantly on his own – then thinks better of it and places it on Bert's.

'Yes?' I ask.

'Yes,' Basti sighs. 'Resistance is futile. You lot, you lot.'

'Yippeeeee!' we all exclaim.

'Come on, the window.' Scruff's now pulling both his uncle's arms.

'Twenty seconds and that's it.'

Oh no. The Caddy kids are having none of that. We march our uncle to a window and keep him there,

285

trapped. As luck would have it we've got Dinda right outside, on a tall ladder, looking most un-Dinda-like in a checked apron and high heels (leopard print) and a matching handkerchief around her head. She's briskly scrubbing a pane of glass next to an extremely dashing man from down the road. He shakes each of our hands.

'Captain McAuliffe – Ian to you and me. Delighted to be of your aquaintance. Delighted indeed!'

He's feverishly painting the window frames. Has just returned from the war himself. When he sees Basti his eyes light up and he gives the older man the most respectful, most heartfelt salute.

Basti's eyes widen. He steps back in shock. 'But I'm a terrible embarrassment . . . aren't I?' He looks at me in bewilderment. 'None of them want me here.'

'Actually,' I say, 'they couldn't think of anything more horrible than you being taken away from this Square. On Christmas Eve, of all nights. You're a big part of it, Basti. You're a legend. A hero. Just like a lot of other people around here. And you know what? They want to help.'

Scruff flings up the window and shouts to all the neighbours swarming over the house. 'You're doing this for Basti Caddy, aren't you? He needs to hear it with his own ears!'

'Yes!' they cry out, 'yes!'

'Basti, welcome back, old man.'

'Jolly good show!'

'We expect a tree to be climbed before tonight.'

'Just trust us, mister.' Dinda smiles the most beautiful smile, right at him, the ghost of a fifteen year old in it from long, long ago. 'Just trust us, you, for once.'

'Three cheers for Mr Caddy!' Captain McAuliffe yells.

And Uncle Basti?

Well, let's just say that at this very moment, with the cheering all around him, it looks like he could almost burst into light.

With happiness.

26
A MOST UNEXPECTED CHRISTMAS PRESENT

The night before Christmas and not a creature stirring, not even a mouse.

And look! Look! At Campden Hill Square. All its tall buildings, its squat chimneys, its green lamp-posts. And in every single window, in every single house, right up to the sky – is a candle.

Lit.

Twinkling at each other, right around the square. Neighbour to neighbour, house to house. It's the most magical, beautiful, enchanting sight. And it's extra special this time around because for the past six years London's been in a grim wartime blackout, and the candles have stayed unlit. But now the gruelling hardship is over. Finally. The city's children have returned from their country exile, the heavy curtains have been taken down, the bomb shelters cleared, the toy factories fired up, the train stations returned to their rightful use. So just imagine it, on this night, December 24th, 1945: the *light*. (And let's never forget the first time that the people of Campden Hill Square had done this. The reason why. The big hearts, the fierce sense of justice, the tolerance. Way back when the trail was blazed: the lights of kindness and community, no matter who you were or where you'd come from.)

Now look at this: all the angry policemen, specialists roped in from out of town, pulling up in their vans and spilling out. Looking terribly determined in their belted suits and hats, faces grim, batons raised in readiness; they're going to find this mysterious Reptilarium and shut it down no matter what. Clear it out. Cart the owner away. Grab the children. Entirely dismantle the house. Just like that!

The policemen run up the hill and across the streets, through the snow-wrapped garden, along the icy pavements, up and down and back again. Trying to find a clue, any clue, to this legendary house they've just been told is so obvious, so sad and lonely and unloved – and crucially – dark.

But you know what?

They never find it.

Because every single house in the square looks incredibly clean and smart, and every single house has its windows lit.

By candles, twinkling in the frosty quiet.

And every time the police rap on a door and ask about the wild, evil man in their midst who's putting all their beleaguered lives most terribly at stake, the owners shake their heads and say no, not here, not this square, absolutely not.

And don't you worry about those four crazy Caddy kids transplanted most cruelly from their beloved house. Oh no. Because you wouldn't believe it. Every other child in the square has decided to donate one of their own Christmas gifts, from under their own trees. But even more wondrously, every child in the square has decided to be their friend. And most gloriously, there are rather a lot of children who live in Campden Hill Square.

So in the fading light of Christmas Eve four kids from the desert on the bottom of the world end up on all manner of sleds and crates, in the wondrous snow that they've never before seen. End up making snowmen and throwing snowballs at just about everyone in sight amid big blousy drops of chilly wet. And that night they excitedly count up a rather obscene amount of Christmas presents, in fact; more than they've ever had in their lives. When all they were expecting was mouse-tail spaghetti and dead rats!

And do you know where they place the gifts, in preparation for Christmas morning?

Right under the golden cage of Perdita, who's looking at all the crazy people in her Reptilarium – especially her Basti, who's quite suddenly flushed – with those eyes as knowing as a cat's.

And some of the mothers and the fathers of the square have promised that when Father Christmas comes, later that night, he'll be directed straight to the Kensington Reptilarium, where – apparently – there are four extremely deserving and helpful and wonderfully kind children, fast asleep. In a bath, a library, and a four-poster bed. Well, they hope. Pin, are you listening? Pin? *Pin?* No disappearing on us any more, all right? That goes for you, too, Bert.

And the grandest turkey feast is planned for tomorrow. Dinda's supplying the roast. Guests of honour: four kids. Species: *Childus Australis Desertus*. Their uncle: the war hero to everyone who's there. Who's said, actually, that perhaps he'd like to see a little more of his neighbour now that his world seems to be sorting itself out – it's a chink of light at last – and it's spoken with the most beautiful smile they've ever seen in their lives.

Also coming: one extremely chuffed Horatio Smythe-Hippet, who's been assured that all reptiles in the vicinity will be most firmly locked up. He's to be accompanied by the bewitching and freshly divorced Mrs Henrietta Witchum Maggs. 'Ahem,' chuckles Basti, every time it's mentioned, 'ahem.'

As well as twenty-five coveted bananas from Charlie Boo's mysterious contacts – and don't worry, there are twenty-five more, one for every person who'll be crammed around his own table at the legendary Bethnal Green Insectarium, for his annual, extremely squashed, but incredibly jolly Christmas feast.

But wait . . . there's one more thing . . . the most incredible thing of the lot –

27
BASTI'S
SURPRISE

The doorbell.

In the middle of an extremely raucous Christmas feast. Me in a dress, of all things – yes a dress, styled by Berti of Kensington, no less – and who would have thought.

'Who could *that* be?' Dinda asks. 'I'm not expecting anyone else.'

We all run to the door.

Hear a bark.

A *bark*?

No. Look at each other.

My heart leaps.

I look at Basti. He nods, smiling most mysteriously, full of chuff. I burst open the door. I know that bark, know it anywhere.

Bucket – *Bucket!* – leaps into my arms.

Knocks me over with her joy and almost licks me to death and us kids pile on top of her in one big squealy, licky, laughy, squirmy mess. Bucket, Bucket, our dear, lovely girl!

And then . . . and then . . . I look up.

To someone behind our dog.

Who's transported her to us. All the way across the world.

Who we didn't even notice in the excitement.

Who's so terribly thin. And faded. Like a ghost. Half human, a skeleton, not quite real.

But no, he's not a ghost at all.

The man steps back. Smiles. Holds out his arms, shakes his head. I bite my lip. He looks . . . familiar. Kind of. No. He's so thin? Pale? Snowy hair, completely, utterly white. Like he's been through such an awful lot. Could it be?

Yes. Yes. Yes.

I start to cry, for the first time in so long, big gulping galumphing sobs.

The skeleton man smiles. His mouth is trembling. I've never seen that in a man before. I run into his arms. Dad. Dad. My beautiful daddy. Back. He holds me and holds me and squeezes me tight, as if he's never, *ever*, going to let me go.

'Kicketty. My girl,' he whispers. 'And all dolled up! Who would have thought.'

Dad.

Who we never thought was coming back, who we'd given up on.

Berti and Scruff turn from Bucket, wondering what on earth I'm doing. Stare at their big sister sobbing in a strange man's arms. Then it dawns. Scruff rushes forward and leaps at Dad with a scream.

'Daddeeeeeeeeeeeeee!'

The three of us fall flat on the ground in a huge, laughing heap; then Bert joins in, then Pin.

'*This*, my friends, is why I had to do Christmas on my own terms,' Basti says, his hands frozen at his cheeks in delight and wonderment. 'I had a Christmas present all arranged, you see. The biggest surprise of the lot. I didn't want it spoilt. Couldn't.'

So. The best Christmas we ever had, in our lives. A father returned. Who had gone away on a top-secret mission that went horribly wrong. Who ended up in a prisoner-of-war camp in deepest Borneo and escaped while injured; then spent months in the jungle, lost. He was presumed dead, his next of kin was informed. A casualty of the war effort whose whereabouts were unknown. Amnesiac, barely surviving. But then one amazing day . . . he stumbled out.

And now he's back. Courtesy of Basti, his next of kin, who was informed before anyone else. Who had a grand plan to give his nieces and nephews the most suprising Christmas present of their lives – a magical day that they'd never forget. Who rescued his brother's station from the bank, dispatched his plane, and flew him out. With the family's beloved dog, Bucket, by his brother's side, of course.

Uncle Basti. Who would have thought.

He catches my eye.

'I do it my way. As you must, Kick. Never be talked out of it.' And he winks.

AFTERWORD

So that's it. Who I was once. Such a fierce, funny little thing; Kick by name and by nature. And there we all were, celebrating the most amazing, surprising Christmas we'd ever had – with a father who came back. And it was a Christmas that up until the last minute Ralph, Albertina, Phineas and I never thought we'd get.

And do you know what?

The tradition of the candles, in the windows of Campden Hill Square, continues to this very day. And if you walk around that beautiful part of London on the night before Christmas, looking up at all the tall houses with their candles lit, I can tell you that one of them still holds the remnants of the Kensington Reptilarium – but you'll never find out which.

Because the neighbours won't tell you.

It's their secret, all right?

Sssssssh.

AUTHOR'S NOTE

Forgive me, dear reader, for my mind is hazy now and there is one thing I have tweaked in my *Kensington Reptilarium*. Call it the storyteller's deliciousness, if you will. The glorious School of the Air, which brought education to so many children of the Australian outback – and still does – started a few years after my tale begins. But I couldn't resist slipping just a snippet of it in. I so wanted you to know about it, even if those Caddy kids were somewhat unruly recipients of its ingeniousness. For this little cheekiness, I beg your forgiveness. Thank you.

– N.J. Gemmell